FIRST COMES
BABY...

FIRST COMES BABY...

BY

MICHELLE DOUGLAS

First published in Great Britain 2013
by Mills & Boon, an imprint of Harlequin (UK) Limited.
Large Print edition 2013
Harlequin (UK) Limited, Eton House,
18-24 Paradise Road, Richmond, Surrey TW9 1SR

© Michelle Douglas 2013

ISBN: 978 0 263 23686 6

Harlequin (UK) policy is to use papers that are natural,
renewable and recyclable products and made from
wood grown in sustainable forests. The logging and
manufacturing process conform to the legal environmental
regulations of the country of origin.

Printed and bound in Great Britain
by CPI Antony Rowe, Chippenham, Wiltshire

To my editor, Sally Williamson, for her keen editorial eye and all her support.

Many, many thanks.

CHAPTER ONE

'BEN, WOULD YOU consider being my sperm donor?'

Ben Sullivan's head rocked back at his best friend's question. He thrust his glass of wine to the coffee table before he spilled its contents all over the floor, and spun to face her. Meg held up her hand as if she expected him to interrupt her.

Interrupt her?

He coughed. Choked. He couldn't breathe, let alone interrupt her! When he'd demanded to know what was on her mind this wasn't what he'd been expecting. Not by a long shot. He'd thought it would be something to do Elsie or her father, but...

He collapsed onto the sofa and wedged himself in tight against the arm. Briefly, cravenly, he wished himself back in Mexico instead of here in Fingal Bay.

A sperm donor? Him?

A giant hand reached out to seize him around the chest, squeezing every last atom of air out of his lungs. A loud buzzing roared in his ears.

'Let me tell you first why I'd like you as my donor, and then what I see as your role in the baby's life.'

Her no-nonsense tone helped alleviate the pressure in his chest. The buzzing started to recede. He shot forward and stabbed a finger at her. 'Why in God's name do you need a sperm donor? Why are you pursuing IVF at all? You're not even thirty!' She was twenty-eight, like him. 'There's loads of time.'

'No, there's not.'

Everything inside him stilled.

She took a seat at the other end of the sofa and swallowed. He watched the bob of her throat and his hands clenched. She tried to smile but the effort it cost her hurt him.

'My doctor has told me I'm in danger of becoming infertile.'

Bile burned his throat. Meg had always wanted kids. She owned a childcare centre, for heaven's sake. She'd be a great mum. It took an enormous force of will to bite back the angry torrent that burned his throat. Railing at fate wouldn't help her.

'I'm booking in to have IVF so I can fall pregnant asap.'

Hence the reason she was asking him if he'd

be her sperm donor. *Him*? He still couldn't get his head around it. But…'You'll make a brilliant mum, Meg.'

'Thank you.' Her smile was a touch shy. It was the kind of smile that could turn the screws on a guy. 'Not everyone will be as understanding, I fear, but…' She leaned towards him, her blonde hair brushing her shoulders. 'I'm not scared of being a single mum, and financially I'm doing very well. I have no doubt of my ability to look after not only myself but whoever else should come along.'

Neither did he. He'd meant it when he'd said she'd be a great mother. She wouldn't be cold and aloof. She'd love her child. She'd fill his or her days with love and laughter, and it would never have a moment's doubt about how much it was cherished.

His chest burned. An ache started up behind his eyes. She'd give her child the kind of childhood they had both craved.

Meg straightened. 'Now, listen. For the record, if you hate the idea, if it makes you the slightest bit uncomfortable, then we just drop the subject, okay?'

His heart started to thud.

'Ben?'

She had her bossy-boots voice on and it almost made him smile. He gave a hard nod. 'Right.'

'Right.' Her hands twisted together and she dragged in a deep breath. Her knuckles turned white. Ben's heart thumped harder.

'Ben, you're my dearest friend. I trust you with my life. So it somehow only seems right to trust you with another life—a life that will be so important to me.'

He closed his eyes and hauled in more air.

'You're healthy, fit and intelligent—everything I want for my child.'

He opened his eyes again.

She grinned. 'And, while you will never, ever get me to admit this in front of another living soul, there isn't another man whose genes I admire more.'

Behind the grin he sensed her sincerity. And, just like every other time he visited, Meg managed to melt the hardness that had grown in him while he'd been away jetting around the world.

'I want a baby so badly I ache with it.' Her smile faded. 'But having a baby like this—through IVF—there really isn't anyone else to share the journey with me. And an anonymous donor...' She glanced down at her hands. 'I don't know—it just seems a bit cold-blooded, that's all. But if that donor were you, knowing you were a part of it…'

She met his gaze. He read in her face how much this meant to her.

'Well, that wouldn't be so bad, you know? I mean, when my child eventually asks about its father I'll at least be able to answer his or her questions.'

Yeah, but *he'd* be that father. He ran a finger around the collar of his tee shirt 'What kind of questions?'

'Hair colour, eye colour. If you were fun, if you were kind.' She pulled in a breath. 'Look, let me make it clear that I know you have absolutely no desire to settle down, and I know you've never wanted kids. That's not what I'm asking of you. I'm not asking you for any kind of commitment. I see your role as favourite uncle and nothing more.'

She stared at him for a moment. 'I know you, Ben. I promise your name won't appear on the birth certificate unless you want to. I promise the child will never know your identity. Also,' she added, 'I would absolutely die if you were to offer me any kind of financial assistance.'

That made him smile. Meg was darn independent—he'd give her that. Independent *and* bossy.

He suspected she probably thought she made more money than him too.

The fact was neither one of them was crying poor.

'I know that whether you agree to my proposition or not you'll love and support any child of mine the way you love and support me.'

That was true.

She stared at him in a way that suddenly made him want to fidget.

She curled her legs beneath her. 'I can see there's something you want to say. Please, I know this is a big ask so don't hold back.'

Her words didn't surprise him. There'd never been any games between him and Meg. Ben didn't rate family—not his mother, not his father and not his grandmother. Oh, he understood he owed his grandmother. Meg lectured him about it every time he was home, and she was right. Elsie had fed, clothed and housed him, had made sure he'd gone to school and visited the doctor when he was sick, but she'd done it all without any visible signs of pleasure. His visits now didn't seem to give her any pleasure either. They were merely a duty on both sides.

He'd make sure she never wanted for anything

in her old age, but as far as he was concerned that was where his responsibility to her ended. He only visited her to make Meg happy.

He mightn't rate family, but he rated friendship—and Meg was the best friend he had. Megan Parrish had saved him. She'd taken one look at his ten-year-old self, newly abandoned on Elsie's doorstep, and had announced that from that day forth they were to be best friends for ever. She'd given his starved heart all the companionship, loyalty and love it had needed. She'd nurtured them both with fairytales about families who loved one another; and with the things they'd do, the adventures they'd have, when they grew up.

She'd jogged beside him when nothing else would ease the burn in his soul. He'd swum beside her when nothing else would do for her but to immerse herself in an underwater world—where she would swim for as long as she could before coming up for air.

And he'd watched more than once as she'd suffered the crippling agony of endometriosis. Nothing in all his life had ever made him feel so helpless as to witness her pain and be unable to ease it. His hands clenched. He hadn't realised she still suffered from it.

'Ben?'

'I'm concerned about your health.' Wouldn't her getting pregnant be an unnecessary risk at this point? 'That's what I want to talk about.'

He shifted on the sofa to survey her more fully. She held her glass out and he topped it up from the bottle of Chardonnay they'd opened during dinner. Her hand shook and something inside him clenched. He slammed the bottle to the coffee table. 'Are you okay?' he barked without preamble.

She eyed him over the glass as she took a sip. 'Yes.'

His tension eased. She wouldn't lie to him. 'But?'

'But it's a monthly problem.' She shrugged. 'You know that.'

But he'd thought she'd grown out of it!

Because that's what you wanted to think.

His hands fisted. 'Is there anything I can do?'

Her face softened in the dim light and he wanted to reach across and pull her into his arms and just hold her...breathe her in, press all of his good health and vitality into her body so she would never be sick again. 'No doubt Elsie's told you that I've had a couple of severe bouts of endometriosis over the last few months?'

His stomach rolled and roiled. He nodded. When

he'd roared into town on his bike earlier in the day Meg had immediately sent him next door to duty-visit his grandmother, even though they all knew he only returned to Fingal Bay to visit Meg. Elsie's two topics of conversation had been Meg's health and Meg's father's health. The news had been chafing at him ever since.

'Is the endometriosis the reason you're in danger of becoming infertile?'

'Yes.' She sat back, but her knuckles had turned white again. 'Which is why I'm lusting after your genes and...'

'And?' His voice came out hoarse. How could fate do this to his best friend?

'I don't know what to call it. Maybe there isn't actually a term for it, but it seems somehow wrong to create a child with an anonymous person. So, I want your in-their-prime genes and your lack of anonymity.'

Holding her gaze, he rested his elbows on his knees. 'No fathering responsibilities at all?'

'God, no! If I thought for one moment you felt pressured in that direction I'd end this discussion now.'

And have a baby with an anonymous donor? He could see she would, but he could also see there'd always be a worry at the back of her mind. A fear of the unknown and what it could bring.

There was one very simple reason why Meg had turned to him—she trusted him. And he trusted her. She knew him, and knew how deftly he avoided commitment of any kind. She knew precisely what she was asking. And what she'd be getting if he went along with this scheme of hers.

If he agreed to be her sperm donor it would be him helping her become a mother. End of story. It wouldn't be his child. It would be Meg's.

Still, he knew Meg. He knew she'd risk her own health in an attempt to fall pregnant and then carry the child full term and give birth to it. Everything inside him wanted to weep at the thought of her never becoming a mother, but he couldn't be party to her risking her health further. He dragged a hand back through his hair and tried to find the words he needed.

'I will tell you something, though, that is far less admirable.' She sank back against the arm of the sofa and stretched her legs out until one of them touched his knee. 'I'm seriously looking forward to not having endometriosis.'

It took a moment for her words to reach him. He'd been too intent on studying the shape of her leg. And just like that he found himself transported to that moment ten years ago when he'd realised just how beautiful Meg had become. A moment that had started out as an attempt at comfort and turned passionate. In the blink of an eye.

The memory made him go cold all over. He'd thought he'd banished that memory from his mind for ever. That night he'd almost made the biggest mistake of his whole sorry life and risked destroying the only thing that meant anything to him—Meg's friendship. He shook his head, his heart suddenly pounding. It was stupid to remember it now. *Forget it!*

And then her words reached him. He leaned forward, careful not to touch her. 'What did you just say about the endometriosis?'

'You can't get endometriosis while you're pregnant. Pregnancy may even cure me of it.'

If he did what she asked, if he helped her get pregnant, she might never get endometriosis again.

He almost hollered out his assent before self-preservation kicked in. Not that he needed protecting from Meg, but he wanted them on the same page before he agreed to her plan.

'Let me just get this straight. I want to make sure we're working on the same assumptions here.

If I agree to be your sperm donor I'd want to be completely anonymous. I wouldn't want anyone to know. I wouldn't want the child to ever know. Just like it wouldn't if you'd gone through a sperm bank.'

'Not all sperm banks are anonymous.' She shrugged. 'But I figured you'd want anonymity.'

She had that right. If the child knew who its father was it would have expectations. He didn't *do* expectations.

'And this is *your* baby, Meg. The only thing I'd be doing is donating sperm, right?'

'Absolutely.'

'I'd be Uncle Ben, nothing more?'

'Nothing more.'

He opened and closed his hands. Meg would be a brilliant mother and she deserved every opportunity of making that dream come true. She wasn't asking for more than he could give.

He stood. 'Yes,' he said. 'I'll help out any way I can.'

Meg leapt to her feet. Her heart pounded so hard and grew so big in her chest she thought she might take off into the air.

When she didn't, she leapt forward and threw

her arms around all six-feet-three-inches of honed male muscle that was her dearest friend in the world. 'Thank you, Ben! Thank you!'

Dear, *dear* Ben.

She pulled back when his heat slammed into her, immediately reminded of the vitality and utter life contained by all that honed muscle and hot flesh. A reminder that hit her afresh during each and every one of Ben's brief visits.

Her pulse gave a funny little skip and she hugged herself. A baby!

Nevertheless, she made herself step back and swallow the excess of her excitement. 'Are you sure you don't want to take some time to think it over?' She had no intention of railroading him into a decision as important as this. She wanted—needed—him to be comfortable and at peace with this decision.

'He shook his head. 'I know everything I need to. Plus I know you'll be a great mum. And you know everything you need to about me. If you're happy to be a single parent, then I'm happy to help you out.'

She hugged herself again. She knew her grin must be stupidly broad, but she couldn't help it. 'You don't know what this means to me.'

'Yes, I do.'

Yes, he probably did. His answering grin made her stomach soften, and the memory of their one illicit kiss stole through her—as it usually did when emotions ran high between the two of them. She bit back a sigh. She'd done her best to forget that kiss, but ten years had passed and still she remembered it.

She stiffened. Not that she wanted to repeat it!

Good Lord! If things had got out of control that night, as they'd almost threatened to, they'd—

She suppressed a shudder. Well, for one thing they wouldn't be having this conversation now. In fact she'd probably never have clapped eyes on Ben again.

She swallowed her sudden nausea. 'How's the jet lag?' She made her voice deliberately brisk.

He folded his arms and hitched up his chin. It emphasised the shadow on his jaw. Emphasised the disreputable bad-boy languor—the cocky swing to his shoulders and the loose-limbed ease of his hips. 'I keep telling you, I don't get jet lag. One day you'll believe me.'

He grinned the slow grin that had knocked more women than she could count off their feet.

But not her.

She shook her head. She had no idea how he managed to slip in and out of different time zones so easily. 'I made a cheese and fruit platter, if you're interested, and I know it's only spring, and still cool, but as it's nearly a full moon I thought we could sit out on the veranda and admire the view.'

He shrugged with lazy ease. 'Sounds good to me.'

They moved to the padded chairs on the veranda. In the moonlight the arc of the bay glowed silver and the lights on the water winked and shimmered. Meg drew a breath of salt-laced air into her lungs. The night air cooled the overheated skin of her cheeks and neck, and eventually helped to slow the crazy racing of her pulse.

But her heart remained large and swollen in her chest. A baby!

'Elsie said your father's been ill?'

That brought her back to earth with a thump. She sliced off a piece of Camembert and nodded.

He frowned. The moonlight was brighter than the lamp-only light of the living room they'd just retired from, and she could see each and every one of his emotions clearly—primarily frustration and concern for her.

'Elsie said he'd had a kidney infection.'

Both she and Ben called his grandmother by her given name. Not Grandma, or Nanna, or even an honorary Aunt Elsie. It was what she preferred.

Meg bit back a sigh. 'It was awful.' It was pointless being anything other than honest with Ben, even as she tried to shield him from the worst of her father and Elsie. 'He became frail overnight. I moved back home to look after him for a bit.' She'd given up her apartment in Nelson Bay, but not her job as director of the childcare centre she owned, even if her second-in-command *had* had to step in and take charge for a week. Moving back home had only ever been meant as a temporary measure.

And it hadn't proved a very successful one. It hadn't drawn father and daughter closer. If anything her father had only retreated further. However, it had ensured he'd received three square meals a day and taken his medication.

'How is he now?'

'It took him a couple of months, but he's fit as a fiddle again. He's moved into a small apartment in Nelson Bay. He said he wanted to be closer to the amenities—the doctor, the shops, the bowling club.'

Nelson Bay was ten minutes away and the main metropolitan centre of Port Stephens. Fingal Bay crouched at Port Stephens' south-eastern edge—a small seaside community that was pretty and un-spoilt. It was where she and Ben had grown up.

She loved it.

Ben didn't.

'Though I have a feeling that was just an excuse and he simply couldn't stand being in the same house as his only daughter any longer.'

Ben's glass halted halfway to his mouth and he swore at whatever he saw in her face. 'Hell, Meg, why do you have to take this stuff so much to heart?'

After all this time. She heard his unspoken rider. She rubbed her chest and stared out at the bay and waited for the ache to recede.

'Anyway—' his frown grew ferocious '—I bet he just didn't want you sacrificing your life to look after him.'

She laughed. Dear Ben. 'You're sure about that, are you?' Ever since Meg's mother had died when she was eight years old her father had… What? Gone missing in action? Given up? Forgotten he had a daughter? Oh, he'd been there physically. He'd continued to work hard and rake in the money. But he'd shut himself off emotionally—even from her, his only child.

When she glanced back at Ben she found him staring out at the bay, lips tight and eyes narrowed to slits. She had a feeling he wasn't taking in the view at all. The ache in her chest didn't go away. 'I don't get them, you know.'

'Me neither.' He didn't turn. 'The difference between you and me, Meg, is that I've given up trying to work them out. I've given up caring.'

She believed the first statement, but not the second. Not for a moment.

He swung to glare at her. 'I think it's time you stopped trying to understand them and caring so much about it all too.'

If only it were that easy. She shrugged and changed the topic. 'How was it today, with Elsie?'

His lip curled. 'The usual garrulous barrel of laughs.'

She winced. When she and Ben had been ten, his mother had dumped him with his grandmother. She'd never returned. She'd never phoned. Not once. Elsie, who had never exactly been lively, had become even less so. Meg couldn't never remember a single instance when Elsie had hugged Ben or showed him the smallest sign of affection. 'Something's going on with the both of them. They've become as thick as thieves.'

'Yeah, I got that feeling too.'

Her father had come to fatherhood late, Elsie had come to motherhood early, and her daughter—Ben's mother—had fallen pregnant young too. All of which made her father and Elsie contemporaries. She shook her head. They still seemed unlikely allies to her.

'But…' Ben shifted on his chair. 'Do we really care?'

Yes, unfortunately she did. Unlike her father, she couldn't turn her feelings off so easily. Unlike Ben, she couldn't bury them so deep they'd never see the light of day again.

Ben clenched a fist. 'You know what gets me? That you're now stuck looking after this monstrosity of a white elephant of a house.'

She stilled. Ben didn't know? 'I'm not precisely stuck with it, Ben. The house is now mine—he gifted it to me. He had the deeds transferred into my name before he left.'

His jaw slackened. 'He what? Why?'

She cut another slice of Camembert, popped it in her mouth and then shrugged. 'Search me.'

He leaned forward. 'And you accepted it?'

She had. And she refused to flinch at the incredulity in his voice. Some sixth sense had told her to, had warned her that something important hinged on her accepting this 'monstrosity of a white elephant of a house', as Ben called it.

'Why?'

She wasn't sure she'd be able to explain it to Ben, though. 'It seemed important to him.'

Dark blue eyes glared into hers. She knew their precise colour, even if she couldn't make it out in the moonlight.

'You're setting yourself up for more disappointment,' he growled.

'Maybe, but now nobody can argue that I don't have enough room to bring up a baby, because I most certainly do.'

He laughed. Just as she'd meant him to. 'Not when you're living in a five-bedroom mansion with a formal living room, a family room, a rumpus and a three car garage,' he agreed.

'But?'

'Hell, it must be a nightmare to clean.'

'It's not so bad.' She grinned. 'Confession time— I have a cleaning lady.'

'Give me a tent any day.'

A tent was definitely more Ben's style.

She straightened. 'You're home for a week, right?' Ben never stayed longer than a week. 'Do you mind if I make us an appointment with my doctor for Wednesday or Thursday?'

'While I'm in Fingal Bay, Meg, I'm yours to command.'

The thing was, he meant it. Her heart swelled even more. 'Thank you.' She stared at him and something inside her stirred. She shook it away and helped herself to more cheese, forced herself to stare out at the bay. 'Now, you've told me how you ended up in Mexico when I thought you were leading a tour group to Machu Picchu, but where are you heading to next?'

Ben led adventure tours all around the world. He worked on a contract basis for multiple tour companies. He was in demand too, which meant he got to pick and choose where he went and what he did.

'The ski fields of Canada.'

He outlined his upcoming travel plans and his face lit up. Meg wondered what he'd do once he'd seen everything. Start at the beginning again? 'Have you crewed on a yacht sailing around the world yet?'

'Not yet.'

It was the goal on his bucket list he most wanted to achieve. And she didn't doubt that he eventually would. 'It must take a while to sail around the

world. You sure you could go that long without fe-
male company?'

'Haven't you heard of a girl in every port?'

She laughed. She couldn't help it. The problem
was with Ben it probably wasn't a joke.

Ben never dated a woman for longer than two
weeks. He was careful not to date any woman long
enough for her to become bossy or possessive. She
doubted he ever would. Ben injected brand-new
life into the word footloose. She'd never met anyone so jealous of his freedom, who fought ties and
commitment so fiercely—and not just in his love-
life either.

Her stomach clenched, and then she smiled. It
was the reason he was the perfect candidate.

She gripped her hands together. A baby!

CHAPTER TWO

I'M PREGNANT!!!

The words appeared in large type on Ben's computer screen and a grin wider than the Great St Bernard Pass spread across his face.

Brilliant news, he typed back. *Congratulations!!!*

He signed off as *Uncle Ben*. He frowned at that for a moment, and then hit 'send' with a shake of his head and another grin. It had been a month since his visit home, and now… Meg—a mum-to-be! He slumped in his chair and ran a hand back through his hair. He'd toast her in the bar tonight with the rest of the crew.

He went to switch off his computer but a new e-mail had hit his inbox: *FAVOURITE Uncle Ben! Love, M xxx*

He tried the words out loud. 'Favourite Uncle Ben.' He shook his head again, and with a grin set off into the ice and snow of a Canadian ski slope.

Over the next two months Ben started seeing pregnant women everywhere—in Whistler ski lodges, lazing on the beaches of the Pacific islands, where he'd led a diving expedition, on a layover in Singapore, and in New Zealand before *and* after he led a small team on a six day hike from the Bay of Islands down to Trounson Kauri Park.

Pregnant women were suddenly everywhere, and they filled his line of vision. A maternal baby bulge had taken on the same fascination for him as the deep-sea pearls he collected for himself, the rare species of coral he hunted for research purposes, and his rare sightings of Tasmanian devils in the ancient Tasmanian rainforest. He started striking up conversations with pregnant women— congratulating them on the upcoming addition to their family.

To a woman, each and every one of them beamed back at him, their excitement and the love they already felt for their unborn child a mirror of how he knew Meg would be feeling. Damn it! He needed to find a window in his schedule to get home and see her, to share in her excitement.

In the third month he started hearing horror stories.

He shot off to Africa to lead a three-week safari tour, clapping his hands over his ears and doing all he could to put those stories out of his mind. Meg was healthy. And she was strong too—both emotionally and physically. Not to mention smart. His hand clenched. She'd be fine. Nothing bad would happen to her or the baby.

It wouldn't!

'You want to tell me what's eating you?' Stefan, the director of the tour company Ben was contracted to, demanded of Ben on his second night in Lusaka, Zambia. 'You're as snarly as a lion with a thorn in its paw.'

Ben had worked for Stefan for over five years. They'd formed a friendship based on their shared love of adventure and the great outdoors, but it suddenly struck Ben that he knew nothing about the other man's personal life. 'Do you have any kids, Stefan?'

He hadn't known he'd meant to ask the question until it had shot out of his mouth. Stefan gave him plenty of opportunity to retract it, but Ben merely shoved his shoulders back and waited. That was when Stefan shifted on his bar stool.

'You got some girl knocked up, Ben?'

He hadn't. He rolled his shoulders. At least not in the way Stefan meant. 'My best friend at home is pregnant. She's ecstatic about it, and I've been thrilled for her, but I've started hearing ugly stories.'

'What kind of stories?'

Ben took a gulp of his beer. 'Stories involving morning sickness and how debilitating it can be. Fatigue.' Bile filled his mouth and he slammed his glass down. 'Miscarriages. High blood pressure. Diabetes. Sixty-hour labours!' He spat each word out with all the venom that gnawed at his soul.

His hand clenched. So help him God, if any of those things happened to Meg...

'Being a father is the best thing I've ever done with my life.'

Ben's head rocked up to meet Stefan's gaze. What he saw there made his blood start to pump faster. A crack opened up in his chest. 'How many?' he croaked.

Stefan held up three fingers and Ben's jaw dropped.

Stefan clapped him on the shoulder. 'Sure, mate, there are risks, but I bet you a hundred bucks your friend will be fine. If she's a friend of yours she won't be an airhead, so I bet you'll find she's gone into all this with her eyes wide open.'

Meg had, he suddenly realised. But had he? For a moment the roaring in his ears drowned out the noise of the rowdy bar. It downed out everything. Stefan's lips moved. It took an effort of will to focus on the words emerging from them.

'…and she'll have the hubby and the rest of her family to help her out and give her the support she'll need.'

Ben pinched the bridge of his nose and focused on his breathing. 'She's going to be a single mum.' She had no partner to help her, and as far as family went… Well, that had all gone to hell in a hand basket years ago. Meg's father and Elsie? Fat lot of good they'd be. Meg had no one to help her out, to offer her support. No one. Not even him—the man who'd helped get her pregnant.

A breath whistled out of Stefan. 'Man, that's tough.'

All the same, he found himself bristling on Meg's behalf. 'She'll cope just fine. She's smart and independent and—'

'I'm not talking about the mum-to-be, mate. I'm talking about the baby. I mean it's tough on the baby. A kid deserves to have a mother *and* a father.'

Ben found it suddenly hard to swallow. And breathe. Or speak. 'Why?' he croaked.

'Jeez, Ben, parenting is hard work. When one

person hits the wall the other one can take over. When one gets sick, the other one's there. Besides, it means the kid gets exposed to two different views of the world—two different ways of doing things and two different ways of solving a problem. Having two parents opens up the world more for a child. From where I'm sitting, every kid deserves that.'

Ben's throat went desert-dry. He wanted to moisten it, to down the rest of his beer in one glorious gulp, but his hands had started to shake. He dragged them off the table and into his lap, clenched them. All he could see in his mind's eye was Meg, heavily pregnant with a child that had half his DNA.

When he'd agreed to help her out he hadn't known he'd feel this…*responsible.*

'But all that aside,' Stefan continued, 'a baby deserves to be loved unconditionally by the two people who created it. I know I'm talking about an ideal world, here, Ben, but…I just think every kid deserves that love.'

The kind of love he and Meg hadn't received.

The kind of love he was denying his child.

He swiped a hand in front of his face. No! *Her* child!

'You'll understand one day, when you have your own kids, mate.'

'I'm never—'

He couldn't finish the sentence. Because he *was*, wasn't he? He was about to become a father. And he knew in his bones with a clarity that stole his breath that Uncle Ben would never make up for the lack of a father in his child's life.

His child.

He turned back to Stefan. 'You're going to have to find someone to replace me. I can't lead Thursday's safari.' Three weeks in the heart of Africa? He shook his head. He didn't have that kind of time to spare. He had to get home and make sure Meg was all right.

He had to get home and make sure the baby was all right.

CHAPTER THREE

A MOTORBIKE TURNED in at the end of the street. Meg glanced up from weeding the garden and listened. That motorbike sounded just like Ben's, though it couldn't be. He wasn't due back in the country for another seven weeks.

She pressed her hands into the small of her back and stretched as well as she could while still on her knees. This house that her father had given her took a lot of maintenance—more than her little apartment ever had. She'd blocked out Saturday mornings for gardening, but something was going to have to give before the baby came. She just wouldn't have time for the upkeep on this kind of garden then.

She glanced down at her very small baby bump and a thrill shot through her. She rested a hand against it—*her baby*—and all felt right with the world.

And then the motorbike stopped. Right outside her house.

She leapt up and charged around to the front of the house, a different kind of grin building inside her. Ben? One glance at the rangy broad-shouldered frame confirmed it.

Still straddling his bike, he pulled off his helmet and shook out his too-long blond-streaked hair. He stretched his neck first to the left and then to the right before catching sight of her. He stilled, and then the slow grin that hooked up one side of his face lit him up from the inside out and hit her with its impact.

Good Lord. She stumbled. No wonder so many women had fallen for him over the years—he was gorgeous! She knew him so well that his physical appearance barely registered with her these days.

Except...

Except when his smile slipped and she read the uncertainty in his face. Her heart flooded with warmth. This was the first time he'd seen her since she'd become pregnant. Was he worried she wouldn't keep her word? That she'd expect more from him than he was willing or able to give?

She stifled a snort. *As if!*

While she normally delighted in teasing him—and this was an opportunity almost too good to pass up—he had made this dream of hers possi-

ble. It was only fair to lay his fears to rest as soon
as she could.

With mock-seductive slowness she pulled off her
gardening gloves one finger at a time and tossed
them over her shoulder, and then she sashayed
down the garden path and out the gate to where
he still straddled his bike. She pulled her T-shirt
tight across her belly and turned side-on so he
could view it in all its glory.

'Hello, *Uncle Ben*. I'd like you to meet *my baby*
bump—affectionately known as the Munchkin.'

She emphasised the words 'Uncle Ben' and 'my',
so he'd know everything remained the same—that
she hadn't changed her mind and was now expecting more from him than he could give. He should
have more faith in her. She knew him. *Really* knew
him. But she forgave him his fears. Ben and family? That'd be the day.

He stared at her, frozen. He didn't say anything.
She straightened and folded her arms. 'What you're
supposed to say, *Uncle Ben*, is that you're very
pleased to meet said baby bump. And then you
should enquire after my health.'

His head jerked up at her words. 'How are—?'
He blinked. His brows drew together until he was

practically glaring at her. 'Hell, Meg, you look great! As in *really* great.'

'I feel great too.' Pregnancy agreed with her. Ben wasn't the only one to notice. She'd received a lot of compliments over the last couple of months. She stuck out a hip. 'What? Are you saying I was a right hag before?'

'Of course not, I—'

'Ha! Got you.'

But he didn't laugh. She leaned forward to peer into his face, took in the two days' worth of stubble and the dark circles under his eyes. Where on earth had he flown in from? 'How long since you had any sleep?' She shuddered at the thought of him riding on the freeway from Sydney on that bike of his. Ben took risks. He always had. But some of those risks were unnecessary.

His eyes had lowered to her abdomen again.

She tugged on his arm. 'C'mon, Ben. Shower and then sleep.'

'No.'

He didn't move. Beneath his leathers his arm flexed in rock-hardness. She let it go and stepped back. 'But you look a wreck.'

'I need to talk to you.'

His eyes hadn't lifted from her abdomen and she

suddenly wanted to cover herself from his gaze. She brushed a hand across her eyes. *Get a grip. This is Ben.* The pregnancy hormones might have given her skin a lovely glow, but she was discovering they could make her emotionally weird at times too.

'Then surely talking over a cup of coffee makes more sense than standing out here and giving the neighbours something to talk about.'

Frankly, Meg didn't care what any of the neighbours thought, and she doubted any of them, except perhaps for Elsie, gave two hoots about her and Ben. She just wanted him off that bike.

'You look as if you could do with a hot breakfast,' she added as a tempter. A glance at the sun told her it would be a late breakfast.

Finally Ben lifted one leg over the bike and came to stand beside her. She slipped her arm through his and led him towards the front door. She quickly assessed her schedule for the following week— there was nothing she couldn't cancel. 'How long are you home for this time, Uncle Ben?' She kept her voice light because she could feel the tension in him.

'No!' The word growled out of him as he pulled out of her grasp.

She blinked. What had she said wrong?

'I can't do this, Meg.'

Couldn't do what?

He leaned down until his face was level with hers. The light in his eyes blazed out at her. 'Not Uncle Ben, Meg, but Dad. I'm that baby's father.' He reached out and laid a hand across her stomach. '*Its father*. That's what I've got to talk to you about, because father is the role I want to take in its life.'

The heat from his hand burned like a brand. She shoved it away. Stepped back.

He straightened. 'I'm sorry. I know it's not what I agreed to. But—'

'Its father?' she hissed at him, her back rigid and her heart surging and crashing in her chest. The ground beneath her feet was buckling like dangerous surf. 'Damn it, Ben, you collected some sperm in a cup. That doesn't make you a father!'

She reefed open the door and stormed inside. Ben followed hot on her heels. Hot. Heat. His heat beat at her like a living, breathing thing. She pressed a hand to her forehead and kept walking until she reached the kitchen. Sun poured in at all the windows and an ache started up behind her eyes.

She whirled around to him. 'A father? *You?*'

She didn't laugh. She didn't want to hurt him. But Ben—a father? She'd never heard anything more ridiculous. She pressed one hand to her stomach and the other to her forehead again. 'Since when have you ever wanted to be a father?'

He stared back at her, his skin pallid and his gaze stony.

Damn it! How long since he'd slept?

She pushed the thought away. 'Ben, you don't have a single committed bone in your body.' What did he mean to do—hang around long enough to make the baby love him before dashing off to some far-flung corner of the globe? He would build her baby's hopes up just to dash them. He would do that again and again for all of its life—breezing in when it suited him and breezing back out when the idea of family started to suffocate him.

She pressed both hands to her stomach. It was her duty to protect this child. Even against her dearest friend. 'No.' Her voice rang clear in the sunny silence.

He shook his head, his mouth a determined line. 'This is one of the things you can't boss me about. I'm not giving way. I'm the father of the baby you're carrying. There's nothing you can do about that.'

Just for a moment wild hope lifted through her. Maybe they could make this work. In the next moment she shook it off. She'd thought that exact same thing once before—ten years ago, when they'd kissed. *Maybe they could make this work. Maybe she'd be the girl who'd make him stay. Maybe she'd be the girl to defeat his restlessness.* All silly schoolgirl nonsense, of course.

And so was this.

But the longer she stared at him the less she recognised the man in front of her. Her Ben was gone. Replaced by a lean, dark stranger with a hunger in his eyes. An answering hunger started to build through her. She snapped it away, breathing hard, her chest clenching and unclenching like a fist. A storm raged in her throat, blocking it.

'I am going to be a part of this baby's life.'

She whirled back. She would fight him with everything she had.

He leant towards her, his face twisted and dark. 'Don't make me fight you on this. Don't make me fight you for custody, Meg, because I will.'

She froze. For a moment it felt as if even her heart had stopped.

The last of the colour leached from Ben's face.

'Hell.' He backed up a step, and then he turned and bolted.

Meg sprang after him and grabbed his arm just before he reached the back door. She held on for dear life. 'Ben, don't.' She rested her forehead against his shoulder and tried to block a sob. 'Don't look like that. You are not your father.' The father who had—

She couldn't bear to finish that thought. She might not think Ben decent father material, but he wasn't his father either.

'And stop trying to shake me off like that.' She did her best to make her voice crisp and cross. 'If I fall I could hurt the baby.'

He glared. 'That's emotional blackmail.'

'Of the worst kind,' she agreed.

He rolled his eyes, but beneath her hands she felt some of the tension seep out of him. She patted his arm and then backed up a step, uncomfortably aware of his proximity.

'I panicked. You just landed me with a scenario I wouldn't have foreseen in a million years. And you… You don't look like you've slept in days. Neither one of us is precisely firing on all cylinders at the moment.'

He hesitated, but then he nodded, his eyes hooded. 'Okay.'

This wasn't the first time she and Ben had fought. Not by a long shot. One of their biggest had been seven years ago, when Ben had seduced her friend Suzie. Meg had begged him not to. She'd begged Suzie not to fall for Ben's charm. They'd both ignored her.

And, predictably, as soon as Ben had slept with Suzie he'd lost all interest and had been off chasing his next adventure. Suzie had been heartbroken. Suzie had blamed Meg. Man, had Meg bawled him out over *that* one. He'd stayed away from her girlfriends after that.

This fight felt bigger than that one.

Worse still, just like that moment ten years ago—when they'd kissed—it had the potential to destroy their friendship. Instinct told her that. And Ben's friendship meant the world to her.

'So?'

She glanced up to find him studying her intently. 'So…' She straightened. 'You go catch up on some Zs and I'll—'

'Go for a walk along the spit.'

It was where she always went to clear her head. At low tide it was safe to walk all the way along

Fingal Beach and across the sand spit to Fingal Island. It would take about sixty minutes there and back, and she had a feeling she would need every single one of those minutes plus more to get her head around Ben's bombshell.

Her hands opened and closed. She had to find out what had spooked him, and then she needed to un-spook him as quickly as she could. Then life could get back to normal and she could focus on her impending single motherhood.

Single. Solo. She'd sorted it all straight in her mind. She knew what she was doing and how she was going to do it. She would *not* let Ben mess with that.

'Take a water bottle and some fruit. You need to keep hydrated.'

'And you need to eat something halfway healthy before you hit the sack.'

'And we'll meet back here...?'

She glanced at her watch. 'Three o'clock.' That was five hours from now. Enough time for Ben to grab something to eat and catch up on some sleep.

He nodded and then shifted his feet. 'Are you going to make me go to Elsie's?'

She didn't have the energy for another fight. Not

even a minor one. 'There are four guest bedrooms upstairs. Help yourself.'

They'd both started for their figurative separate corners when the doorbell rang. Meg could feel her shoulders literally sag.

Ben shot her a glance. 'I'll deal with it. I'll say you're not available and get rid of whoever it is asap.'

'Thanks.'

She half considered slipping out through the back door while he was gone and making her way down to the bay, but that seemed rude so she made herself remain in the kitchen, her fingers drumming against their opposite numbers.

Her mind whirled. *What on earth was Ben thinking*? She closed her eyes and swallowed. *How on earth was she going to make him see sense*?

'Uh, Meg?'

Her eyes sprang open as Ben returned, his eyes trying to send her some message.

And then Elsie and her father appeared behind him. It took an effort of will to check her surprise. Her father hadn't been in this house since he'd handed her the deeds. And Elsie? Had Elsie *ever* been inside?

Her father thrust out his jaw. 'We want to talk to you.'

She had to bite her lip to stop herself adding please. Her father would resent being corrected. She thrust her jaw out. Well, bad luck, because she resented being spoken to that way and—

'We brought morning tea,' Elsie offered, proffering a bakery bag.

It was so out of character—the whole idea of morning tea, let alone an offering of cake—that all coherent thought momentarily fled.

She hauled her jaw back into place. 'Thank you. Umm...lovely.' And she kicked herself forward to take the proffered bag.

She peeked inside to discover the most amazing sponge and cream concoction topped with rich pink icing. *Yum!* It was the last kind of cake she'd have expected Elsie to choose. It was so frivolous. She'd have pegged Elsie as more of a date roll kind of person, or a plain buttered scone. Not that Meg was complaining. No sirree. This cake was the bee's knees. Her mouth watered. Double *yum*.

She shook herself. 'I'll...um...go and put the percolator on.'

Ben moved towards the doorway. 'I'll make myself scarce.'

'No, Benjamin, it's fortunate you're here,' her father said. 'Elsie rang me when she heard you arrive. That's why we're here. What we have to say will affect you too.'

Ben glanced at Meg. She shrugged. All four of them in the kitchen made everything suddenly awkward. She thought fast. Her father would expect her to serve coffee in the formal lounge room. It was where he'd feel most comfortable.

It was the one room where Ben would feel least comfortable.

'Dad, why don't you and Elsie make yourselves comfortable in the family room? It's so lovely and sunny in there. I'll bring coffee and cake through in a moment.' Before her father could protest she turned to Ben. Getting stuck making small talk with her father and Elsie would be his worst nightmare. 'I'd appreciate it if you could set a tray for me.'

He immediately leapt into action. She turned away to set the percolator going. When she turned back her father and Elsie had moved into the family room.

'What's with them?' Ben murmured.

'I don't know, but I told you last time you were here that something was going down with them.'

They took the coffee and cake into the family room. Meg poured coffee, sliced cake and handed it around.

She took a sip of her decaf and lifted a morsel of cake to her mouth. 'This is *very* good.'

Her father and Elsie sat side by side on the sofa, stiff and formal. They didn't touch their coffee or their cake. They didn't appear to have a slouchy, comfortable bone between them. With a sigh, Meg set her fork on the side of her plate. If she'd been hoping the family room would loosen them up she was sorely disappointed.

She suddenly wanted to shake them! Neither one of them had asked Ben how he was doing, where he'd been, or how long he'd been back. Her hand clenched around her mug. They gave off nothing but a great big blank.

She glanced at Ben. He lounged in the armchair opposite, staring at his cake and gulping coffee. She wanted to shake him too.

She thumped her mug and cake plate down on the coffee table and pasted her brightest smile to her face. She utterly refused to do *blank*. 'While it's lovely to see you both, I get the impression this isn't a social visit. You said there's something you wanted to tell us?'

'That's correct, Megan.'

Her father's name was Lawrence Samuel Parrish. If they didn't call him Mr Parrish—people, that was, colleagues and acquaintances—they called him Laurie. She stared at him and couldn't find even a glimpse of the happy-go-lucky ease that 'Laurie' suggested. Did he resent the familiarity of that casual moniker?

It wasn't the kind of question she could ever ask. They didn't have that kind of a relationship. In fact, when you got right down to brass tacks, she and her father didn't have any kind of relationship worth speaking of.

Her father didn't continue. Elsie didn't take up where he left off. In fact the older woman seemed to be studying the ceiling light fixture. Meg glanced up too, but as far as she could tell there didn't seem to be anything amiss—no ancient cobwebs or dust, and it didn't appear to be in imminent danger of dropping on their heads.

'Well!' She clapped her hands and then rubbed them together. 'We're positively agog with excitement—aren't we, Ben?'

He started. 'We are?'

If she'd been closer she'd have kicked him. 'Yes, of course we are.'

Not.

Hmm... Actually, maybe a bit. This visit really was unprecedented. It was just that this ritual of her doing her best to brisk them up and them steadfastly resisting had become old hat. And suddenly she felt too tired for it.

She stared at *Laurie* and Elsie. They stared back, but said nothing. With a shrug she picked up her mug again, settled back in her *easy* chair and took a sip. She turned to Ben to start a conversation. *Any* conversation.

'Which part of the world have you been jaunting around this time?'

He turned so his body was angled towards her, effectively excluding the older couple. 'On safari in Africa.'

'Lions and elephants?'

'More than you could count.'

'Elsie and I are getting married.'

Meg sprayed the space between her and Ben with coffee. Ben returned the favour. Elsie promptly rose and took their mugs from them as they coughed and coughed. Her father handed them paper napkins. It was the most animated she'd ever seen them. But then they sat side-by-side on the sofa again, as stiff and formal as before.

Meg's coughing eased. She knew she should excuse herself for such disgusting manners, but she didn't. For once she asked what was uppermost in her mind. 'Are you serious?'

Her father remained wooden. 'Yes.'

That was it. A single yes. No explanation. No declaration of love. Nothing.

She glanced at Ben. He was staring at them as if he'd never seen them before. He was staring at them with a kind of fascinated horror, as if they were a car wreck he couldn't drag his gaze from.

She inched forward on her seat, doing all she could to catch first her father's and then Elsie's eyes. 'I don't mean to be impertinent, but...*why*?'

'That *is* impertinent.' Her father's chin lifted. 'And none of your business.'

'If it's not my business then I don't know who else's it is,' she shot back, surprising herself. Normally she was the keeper of the peace, the smoother-over of awkward moments, doing all she could to make things easy for this pair who, it suddenly occurred to her, had never exactly made things easy for either her or Ben.

'I told you they wouldn't approve!' Elsie said.

'Oh, it's not that I don't approve,' Meg managed.

'I don't,' Ben growled.

She stared at him. 'Yeah, but you don't approve of marriage on principle.' She rolled her eyes. Did he seriously think he wanted to be a father?

Think about that later.

She turned back to the older couple. 'The thing is, I didn't even know you were dating. Why the secrecy? And…and…I mean…'

Her father glanced at Elsie and then at Meg. 'What?' he rapped out.

'Do you love each other?'

Elsie glanced away. Her father's mouth opened and closed but no sound came out.

'I mean, surely that's the only good reason to marry, isn't it?'

Nobody said anything. Her lips twisted. *Have a banana, Meg.* Was she the only person in this room who believed in love—good, old-fashioned, rumpy-pumpy love?

'Elsie and I have decided that we'll rub along quite nicely together.'

She started to roll her eyes at her father's pomposity, but then he did something extraordinary— he reached out and clasped Elsie's hand. Elsie held his hand on her lap and it didn't look odd or alien or wrong.

Meg stared at those linked hands and had to

fight down a sudden lump in her throat. 'In that case, congratulations.' She rose and kissed them both on the cheek.

Ben didn't join her.

She took her seat and sent him an uneasy glance. 'Ben?'

He shrugged. 'It's no business of mine.' He lolled in his chair with almost deliberate insolence. 'They're old enough to know what they want.'

'Precisely,' her father snapped.

She rubbed her forehead. No amount of smoothing would ease this awkward moment. She decided to move the moment forward instead. 'So, where will you live?'

'We'll live in my apartment at Nelson Bay.'

She turned to Elsie. 'What will you do with your house?'

Before he'd retired Meg's father had been a property developer. He still had a lot of contacts in the industry. Maybe they'd sell it. Maybe she'd end up with cheerful neighbours who'd wave whenever they saw her and have young children who'd develop lifelong friendships with her child.

'I'm going to give it to Ben.'

Ben shot upright to tower over all of them. 'I don't want it!'

Her father rose. 'That's an ungracious way to respond to such a generous gift.'

Ben glared at his grandmother. 'Is he railroading you into this?'

'Most certainly not!' She stood too. 'Meg's right. She's seen what you haven't—or what you can't. Not that I can blame you for that. But...but Laurie and I love each other. I understand how hard you might find that to believe after the way the two of us have been over the years, but I spent a lot of time with him when he was recuperating.' She shot Meg an almost apologetic glance that made Meg fidget. 'When you were at work, that is. We talked a lot. And we're hoping it's not too late for all of us to become a family,' she finished falteringly, her cheeks pink with self-consciousness.

It was one of the longest speeches Meg had ever heard her utter, but one glance at Ben and she winced.

'A family?' he bellowed.

'Sit!' Meg hollered.

Everyone sat, and then stared at her in varying degrees of astonishment. She marvelled at her own daring, and decided to bluff it out. 'Have you set a date for the wedding?'

Elsie darted a glance at Meg's father. 'We thought the thirtieth of next month.'

Next month? The end of March?

That was only six weeks away!

'We'll be married by a celebrant at the registry office. We'd like you both to be there.' Her father didn't look at her as he spoke.

'Of course.' Though heaven only knew how she'd get Ben there. He avoided weddings like the plague—as if he thought they might somehow be catching.

'And where have you settled on for your honeymoon?'

'I…' He frowned. 'We're too old for a honeymoon.'

She caught his eye. 'Dad, do you love Elsie?'

He swallowed and nodded. She'd never seen him look more vulnerable in his life.

She blinked and swallowed. 'Then you're not too old for a honeymoon.' She hauled in a breath. 'And, like Elsie, are you hoping to rebuild family ties?'

'I sincerely hope so, Megan. I mean, you have a baby on the way now.'

Correction—she'd never seen him look more vulnerable until *now*. He was proffering the olive branch she'd been praying for ever since she was eight years old, and she found all she wanted to do was run from the room. A great ball of hardness lodged in her stomach. Her father was willing to change for a grandchild, but not for *her*.

'Meg.'

She understood the implicit warning Ben sent her. He didn't want her hurt or disappointed. *Again.* She understood then that the chasm between them all might be too wide ever to be breached.

She folded her arms, her brain whirling. Very slowly, out of the mists of confusion and befuddlement—and resentment—a plan started to form. She glanced at the happy couple. A plan perfect in its simplicity. She glanced at Ben. A plan devious in design. *A family, huh?* They'd see about that. All of them. Laurie and Elsie, and Ben too.

She stood and moved across to Ben's chair. 'You must allow Ben and I to throw you a wedding—a proper celebration to honour your public commitment to each other.'

'What the—?'

Ben broke off with a barely smothered curse when she surreptitiously pulled his hair.

'Oh, that's not necessary—' Elsie started.

'Of course it is!' Meg beamed at her. 'It will be our gift to you.'

Her father lumbered to his feet, panic racing across his face. Meg winked at Elsie before he could speak. 'Every woman deserves a wedding day, and my father knows the value of accepting generosity in the spirit it's given. Don't you, Dad?'

Family, huh? Well, he'd have to prove it.

He stared at her, dumbfounded and just a little... afraid? That was when it hit her that all his pomposity and stiffness stemmed from nervousness. He was afraid that she'd reject him. The thought made her flinch. She pushed it away.

'We'll hold the wedding here,' she told them, lifting her chin. 'It'll be a quiet affair, but classy and elegant.'

'I...' Her father blinked.

Ben slouched down further in his chair.

Elsie studied the floor at her feet.

Meg met her father's gaze. 'I believe thank you is the phrase you're looking for.' She sat and lifted the knife. 'More cake, anyone?' She cut Ben another generous slice. 'Eat up, Ben. You're looking a bit peaky. I need you to keep your strength up.'

He glowered at her. But he demolished the cake. After the smallest hesitation, Elsie forked a sliver of cake into her mouth. Her eyes widened. Her head came up. She ate another tiny morsel. Watching her, Laurie did the same.

'What the hell do you think you're doing?' Ben rounded on her the instant the older couple left.

She folded her arms and nodded towards the staircase. 'You want to go take that nap?'

He thrust a finger under her nose. 'What kind of patsy do you take me for? I am *not* helping you organise some godforsaken wedding. You got that?'

Loud and clear.

'The day after tomorrow I'm out of here, and I won't be back for a good three months.'

Exactly what she'd expected.

'Do you hear me, Meg? Can I make myself any clearer?'

'The day after tomorrow, huh?'

'Yes.'

'And you won't be back until around May?'

'Precisely.' He set off towards the stairs.

She folded her arms even tighter. She waited until he'd placed his foot on the first riser. 'So you've given up on the idea of fatherhood, then?'

He froze. And then he swung around and let forth with a word so rude she clapped her hands across her stomach in an attempt to block her un-born baby's ears. *'Ben!'*

'You…' The finger he pointed at her shook.

'I *nothing*,' she shot back at him, her anger rising to match his. 'You can't just storm in here and demand all the rights and privileges of fatherhood unless you're prepared to put in the hard yards. Domesticity and commitment includes dealing with my father and your grandmother. It includes helping out at the odd wedding, attending baptisms and neighbourhood pool parties and all those other things you loathe.'

She strode across to stand directly in front of him. 'Nobody is asking you to put in those hard yards—least of all me.'

His eyes narrowed. 'I know exactly what you're up to.'

He probably did. That was what happened when someone knew you so well.

'You think the idea of helping out at this wedding is going to scare me off.'

She raised an eyebrow. Hadn't it?

'It won't work, Meg.'

They'd see about that. 'Believe me, Ben, a baby is a much scarier proposition than a wedding. Even this wedding.'

'You don't think I'll stick it out?'

Not for a moment. 'If you can't stick the wedding out then I can't see how you'll stick fatherhood out.' And she'd do everything she could to protect her child from that particular heartache. 'End of story.'

The pulse at the base of his jaw thumped and his eyes flashed blue fire. It was sexy as hell.

She blinked and then took a step back. Stupid pregnancy hormones!

He thrust out his hand. 'You have yourself a deal, Meg, and may the best man win.'

She refused to shake it. Her eyes stung. She swallowed a lump the size of a Victorian sponge. 'This isn't some stupid bet, Ben. This is my baby's life!'

His face softened but the fire in his eyes didn't dim. 'Wrong, Meg. Our baby. It's *our* baby's life.'

He reached out and touched the backs of his fingers to her cheek. And then he was gone.

'Oh, Ben,' she whispered after him, reaching up to touch the spot on her cheek that burned from his touch. He had no idea what he'd just let himself in for.

CHAPTER FOUR

BEN SLEPT IN one of Meg's spare bedrooms instead of next door at Elsie's.

He slept the sleep of the dead.

He slept for twenty straight hours.

When he finally woke and traipsed into the kitchen, the first thing he saw was Meg hunched over her laptop at the kitchen table. The sun poured in at the windows, haloing her in gold. She glanced up. She smiled. But it wasn't her regular wide, unguarded smile.

'I wondered when you'd surface.'

He rubbed the back of his neck. 'I can't remember the last time I slept that long.' Or that well.

'Where were you?'

He frowned and pointed. 'Your back bedroom.'

Her grin lit her entire face. 'I meant where exactly in Africa were you before you flew home to Australia?'

Oh, right. 'Zambia, to be exact.' He was supposed to be leading a safari.

She stared at him, but he couldn't tell what she was thinking. He remembered that conversation with Stefan, and the look of fulfilment that had spread across his friend's face when he'd spoken about his children. It had filled Ben with awe, and the sudden recognition of his responsibilities had changed everything.

He had to be a better father than his own had been. He had to or—

His stomach churned and he cut the thought off. It was too early in the day for such grim thoughts.

'Exciting,' she murmured.

He shifted his weight to the balls of his feet. 'Meg, are we okay—you and me?'

'Of course we are.' But she'd gone back to her laptop and she didn't look up as she spoke. When he didn't move she waved a hand towards the pantry. 'Look, we need to talk, but have something to eat first while I finish up these accounts. Then we'll do precisely that.'

He'd stormed in here yesterday and upended all of her plans. Meg liked her ducks in neat straight rows. She liked to know exactly where she was going and what she was working towards. He'd put paid to all of that, and he knew how much it rattled her when her plans went awry.

Awry? His lips twisted. He'd blown them to smithereens. The least he could do was submit to her request with grace, but…

'You're working on a Sunday?'

'I run my own business, Ben. I work when I have to work.'

He shut up after that. It struck him how much Meg stuck to things, and how much *he* never had. As soon as he grew bored with a job or a place he moved on to the next one, abuzz with the novelty and promise of a new experience. His restlessness had become legendary amongst his friends and colleagues. No wonder she didn't have any faith in his potential as a father.

All you did was collect sperm in a cup.

He flinched, spilling cereal all over the bench. With a muffled curse he cleaned it up and then stood, staring out of the kitchen window at the garden beyond while he ate.

You never planned to have a child.

He hadn't. He'd done everything in his power to avoid that kind of commitment. Bile rose in his throat. So what the hell was he doing here?

He stared at the bowl he held and Stefan's face, words, rose in his mind. *A baby deserves both a mother and a father.* He pushed his shoulders back and rinsed his bowl. He might not have planned this, but he had no intention of walking away from his child. He couldn't.

He swung to Meg, but she didn't look up from her computer. He wasn't hungry but he made toast. He ate because he wanted his body clock to adjust to the time zone. He ate to stop himself from demanding that Meg stop what she was doing and talk to him right now.

After he'd washed and dried the dishes Meg turned off her computer and pushed it to one side. He poured two glasses of orange juice and sat down. 'You said we have to talk.' He pushed one of the glasses towards her.

She blinked. 'And you don't think that's necessary?'

'I said what I needed to say yesterday.' He eyed her for a moment. 'And I don't want to fight.'

She stared at him, as if waiting for more. When he remained silent she blew out a breath and shook her head.

He rolled his shoulders and fought a scowl. 'What?'

'You said yesterday that you want to be acknowledged as the baby's father.'

'I do.'

'And that you want to be a part of its life.'

He thrust out his jaw. 'That's right.'

'Then would you kindly outline the practicalities of that for me, please? What precisely are your intentions?'

He stared at her blankly. What was she talking about?

She shook her head again, her lips twisting. 'Does that mean you want to drop in and visit the baby once a week? Or does it mean you want the baby to live with you for two nights a week and every second weekend? Or are you after week-about parenting?' Her eyes suddenly blazed with scorn. 'Or do you mean to flit in and out of its life as you do now, only instead of calling you Uncle Ben the child gets the privilege of calling you Daddy?'

Her scorn almost burned the skin from his face.

She leaned towards him. 'Do you actually mean to settle down and help care for this baby?'

Settle down? His mouth went dry. He hadn't thought…

She drew back and folded her arms. 'Or do you mean to keep going on as you've always done?'

She stared at him, her blazing eyes and the tension in her folded arms demanding an answer.

He had to say something. 'I...I haven't thought the nuts and bolts of the arrangements through.' It wasn't much to give her, but at least it was the truth.

'You can't have it both ways, Ben. You're either globe-trotting Uncle Ben or one hundred per cent involved Daddy. I won't settle for anything but the best for my child.'

He leapt out of his chair. 'You can't demand I change my entire life!'

She stared at him, her eyes shadowed. 'I'm not. I've never had any expectations of you. You're the one who stormed in here yesterday and said you wanted to be a father. And a true father is—'

'More than sperm in a cup.' He fell back into his seat.

She pressed her fingers to her eyes. 'I'm sorry. I put that very crudely yesterday.'

Her guilt raked at him. She hadn't done anything wrong. He was the one who'd waltzed in and overturned her carefully laid plans.

She lifted her head. 'A father is so much more than an uncle, Ben. Being a true father demands more commitment than your current lifestyle allows for. A father isn't just for fun and games. Being a father means staying up all night when your child is sick, running around to soccer and netball games, attending parent and teacher nights.'

His hands clenched. His stomach clenched tighter. He'd stormed in here without really knowing what he was demanding. He still didn't know what he was demanding. He just knew he couldn't walk away.

'Ben, what do you even know about babies?'

Zilch. Other than the fact that they were miracles. And that they deserved all the best life had to give.

'Have you ever held one?'

Nope. Not even once.

'Do you even know how to nurture someone?'

He stiffened. *What the hell...?*

'I don't mean do you know how to lead a group safely and successfully down the Amazon, or to base camp at Everest, or make sure someone attaches the safety harness on their climbing equipment correctly. Do you know how to care for someone who is sick or who's just feeling a bit depressed?'

What kind of selfish sod did she think him?

His mouth dried. What kind of selfish sod *was* he?

'I'm not criticising you. Those things have probably never passed across your radar before.' Her brow furrowed. 'You have this amazing and exciting life. Do you really want to give it up for nappies, teething, car pools and trips to the dentist?'

He couldn't answer that.

'Do you *really* want to be a father, Ben?'

He stared at his hands. He curled his fingers against his palms, forming them into fists. 'I don't know what to do.' He searched Meg's eyes—eyes that had given him answers in the past. 'What should I do?' Did she think he had it in him to become a good father?

'No way!' She shot back in her chair. 'I am not going to tell you what to do. I am not going to make this decision for you. It's too important. This is something you have to work out for yourself, Ben.'

His mouth went drier than the Kalahari Desert. Meg meant to desert him?

Her face softened. 'If you don't want that level of involvement I will understand. You won't be letting me down. We'll carry on as we've always done and there'll be no hard feelings. At least not on my side.'

Or his!

'But if you do want to be a proper father it only

seems fair to warn you that my expectations will be high.'

He swallowed. He didn't *do* expectations.

She reached out and touched his hand. He stared at it and suddenly realised how small it was.

'I'm so grateful to you, Ben. I can't tell you how much I'm looking forward to becoming a mother—how happy I am that I'm pregnant. You helped make that possible for me. If you do want to be a fully involved father I would never deny that to you.'

It was a tiny hand, and as he stared at it he suddenly remembered the fairytales she'd once spun about families—perfect mothers and fathers, beautiful children, loving homes—when the two of them had been nothing but children themselves. She'd had big dreams.

He couldn't walk away. She was carrying *his* child. But could he live up to her expectations of what a father should be? Could he live up to his own expectations? Could he do a better job than his father had done?

His heart thumped against his ribcage. It might be better for all concerned if he got up from this table right now and just walked away.

'I realise this isn't the kind of decision you can make overnight.'

Her voice hauled him back from the brink of an abyss.

'But, Ben, for the baby's sake…and for mine… could you please make your decision by the time the wedding rolls around?'

His head lifted. Six weeks? She was giving him six weeks? If he could cope with six weeks living in Fingal Bay, that was.

He swallowed. If he couldn't he supposed they'd have their answer.

'And speaking of weddings…' She rose and hitched her head towards the back door.

Weddings? He scowled.

'C'mon. I need your help measuring the back yard.'

'What the hell for—?'

He broke off on an expletive to catch the industrial tape measure she tossed him—an old one of her father's, no doubt—before it brained him. She disappeared outside.

Glowering, he slouched after her. 'What for?' he repeated.

'For the marquee. Elsie and my father can be married in the side garden by the rose bushes, weather permitting, and we'll set up a marquee out the back here for the meal and speeches and dancing.'

'Why the hell can't they get married in the registry office?'

She spun around, hands on hips. The sun hit her hair, her eyes, the shine on her lips. With her baby bump, she looked like a golden goddess of fertility. A *desirable* goddess. He blinked and took a step back.

'This is a wedding. It should be celebrated.'

'I have never met two people less likely to want to celebrate.'

'Precisely.'

He narrowed his eyes. 'What are you up to?'

'Shut up, Ben, and measure.'

They measured.

The sun shone, the sky was clear and salt scented the air, mingling with the myriad scents from Meg's garden. Given the sobering discussion they'd just had, he'd have thought it impossible to relax, but as he jotted down the measurements that was exactly what he found himself doing.

To his relief, Meg did too. He knew he'd freaked her out with his announcement yesterday—that he'd shocked and stressed her. He paused. And then stiffened. He'd *stressed* her. She was pregnant and he'd stressed her. He was an idiot! Couldn't he have found a less threatening and shocking way of blurting his intentions out?

His hands clenched. He was a tenfold idiot for not actually working out the nuts and bolts of those intentions prior to bursting in on her the way he had—for not setting before her a carefully thought-out plan that she could work with. She'd spend the next six weeks in a state of uncertainty—which for Meg translated into stress and worry and an endless circling litany of 'what-ifs'—until he made a decision. He bit back a curse. She'd dealt with him with more grace than he deserved.

He shot a quick glance in her direction. She didn't look stressed or fragile or the worse for wear at the moment. Her skin glowed with a health and vigour he'd never noticed before. Her hair shone in the sun and...

He rolled his shoulders and tried to keep his attention above neck level.

It was just... Her baby bump was small, but it was unmistakable. And it fascinated him.

'Shouldn't you be taking it easy?' he blurted out in the middle of some soliloquy she was giving him about round tables versus rectangular.

She broke off to blink at him, and then she laughed. 'I'm pregnant, not ill. I can keep doing all the things I was doing before I became pregnant.'

Yeah, but she was doing a lot—perhaps more than was good for her. She ran her own childcare centre—worked there five days a week and heaven only knew how many other hours she put into it. She had to maintain this enormous house and garden. And now she was organising a wedding.

He folded his arms. It was just as well he had come home. He could at least shoulder some of the burden and make sure she looked after herself. Regardless of any other decision he came to, he could at least do that.

She started talking again and his gaze drifted back towards her baby bump. But on the way down the intriguing shadow of cleavage in the vee of her shirt snagged his attention. His breath jammed in his throat and a pulse pounded at his groin. The soft cotton of her blouse seemed to enhance the sweet fullness of her breasts.

That pulse pounded harder as he imagined the weight of those breasts in his hands and the way the nipples would harden if he were to run his thumbs over them—back and forth, over and over, until her head dropped back and her lips parted and her eyes glazed with desire.

His mouth dried as he imagined slipping the buttons free and easing that blouse from her shoulders, gazing at those magnificent breasts in the sun and dipping his head to—

He snapped away. *Oh, hell!* That was *Meg* he was staring at, lusting after.

He raked both hands back through his hair and paced, keeping his eyes firmly fixed on the ground in front of him. Jet lag—that had to be it. Plus his brain was addled and emotions were running high after the conversation they'd had.

And she was pregnant with *his* child. Surely it was only natural he'd see her differently? He swallowed and kept pacing. Once he'd sorted it all out in his head, worked out what he was going to do, things would return to normal again. His hands unclenched, his breathing eased. Of course it would.

He came back to himself to find her shaking his arm. 'You haven't heard a word I've said, have you? What's wrong?'

Her lips looked plump and full and oh-so-kissable. He swallowed. 'I…uh…' They were measuring the back yard. That was right. 'Where are we going to find enough people to fill this tent of yours?'

'Marquee,' she corrected. 'And I'm going to need your help on that one.'

His help. *Focus on that—not on the way her bottom lip curves or the neckline of her shirt or—*

Keep your eyes above her neck!

'Help?' he croaked, suddenly parched.

'I want you to get the names of ten people Elsie would like to invite to the wedding.'

That snapped him to. 'Me?'

'I'll do the same for my father. I mean to invite some of my friends, along with the entire street. Let me know if there's anyone you'd like to invite too.'

'Dave Clements,' he said automatically. Dave had thrown Ben a lifeline when he'd most needed one. It would be great to catch up with him.

But then he focused on Meg's order again. Ten names from Elsie? She had to be joking right? 'Does she even *know* ten people?'

'She must do. She goes to Housie one afternoon a week.'

She did?

'Who knows? She might like to invite her chiropodist.'

Elsie had a chiropodist?

'But how am I going to get her to give me two names let alone ten?' He and his grandmother could barely manage a conversation about the weather, let alone anything more personal.

'That's your problem. You're supposed to be resourceful, aren't you? What do you do if wild hyenas invade your camp in Africa? Or if your rope starts to unravel when you're rock-climbing? Or your canoe overturns when you're white-water rafting? This should be a piece of cake in comparison.'

Piece of cake, his—

'Besides, I'm kicking you out of my spare room, so I expect you'll have plenty of time to work on her.'

He gaped at her. 'You're not going to let me stay?'

'Your place is over there.' She pointed across the fence. 'For heaven's sake, Ben, she's *giving* that house to you.'

'I don't want it.'

'Then you'd better find a more gracious way of refusing it than that.'

She stood there with hands on hips, eyes flashing, magnificent in the sunlight, and it suddenly occurred to him that moving out of her spare bed-room might be a very good plan. At least until his body clock adjusted.

She must have read the capitulation in his face because her shoulders lost their combativeness. She clasped her hands together and her gaze slid away. He wondered what she was up to now.

'I…um…' She glanced up at him again and swallowed. 'I want to ask you something, but I'm afraid it might offend you—which isn't my intention at all.'

He shrugged. 'Ask away, Meg.'

She bent down and pretended to study a nearby rosebush. He knew it was a pretence because he knew Meg. She glanced at him and then back at the rosebush. 'We're friends, right? Best friends. So that means it's okay to ask each other personal questions, don't you think?'

His curiosity grew. 'Sure.' For heaven's sake, they were having a baby together. How much more personal could it get?

'You really mean to stay in Fingal Bay for the next six weeks?'

'Yes.'

She straightened. 'Then I want to ask if you have enough money to see you through till then. Money

isn't a problem for me, and if you need a loan…'
She trailed off, swallowing. 'I've offended you,
haven't I?'

He had to move away to sit on a nearby bench.
Meg thought him some kind of freeloading loser?
His stomach churned. He pinched the bridge of his
nose. No wonder she questioned his ability to be
any kind of decent father to their child.

'I'm not casting a slur on your life or your masculinity,' she mumbled, sitting beside him, 'but
you live in the moment and go wherever the wind
blows you. Financial security has never been important to you. Owning things has never been important to you.'

He lifted his head to survey the house behind
her. 'And they are to you?' It wasn't the image he
had of her in his mind. But her image of *him* was
skewed. It was just possible they had each other
completely wrong.

After all, how much time had they really spent
in each other's company these last five to seven
years?

She gave a tiny smile and an equally tiny shrug.
'With a baby on the way, financial security has become very important to me.'

'Is that why you let your father gift you this house?'

'No.'

'Then why?' He turned to face her more fully. 'I'd have thought you'd hate this place.' The same way he hated it.

She studied him for a long moment. 'Not all the associations are bad. This is where my mother came as a new bride. This is where I met my best friend.'

Him.

'Those memories are good. And look.' She grabbed his hand and tugged him around the side of the house to the front patio. 'Look at that view.'

She dropped his hand and a part of him wished she hadn't. The crazy mixed-up, jet lagged part.

'This has to be one of the most beautiful places in the world. Why wouldn't I want to wake up to that every day?'

He stared at the view.

'Besides, Fingal Bay is a nice little community. I think it's a great place to raise a child.'

He stared out at the view—at the roofs of the houses on the street below and the curving bay just beyond. The stretch of sand bordering the bay and leading out to the island gleamed gold in the sun. The water sparkled a magical green-blue. He stared at the boats on the water, listened to the cries of the seagulls, the laughter of children, and tried to see it all objectively.

He couldn't. Every rock and curve and bend was imbued with his childhood.

But…

He'd travelled all around the world and Meg was right. The picturesque bay in front of him rivalled any other sight he'd seen.

He turned to her. 'It's as simple as that? This is where you want to live so you accepted this house as a gift?'

A sigh whispered out of her, mingling with the sounds of the waves whooshing up onto the sand. 'It's a whole lot more complicated than that. It was as if…as if my father *needed* to give me this house.'

He leant towards her. 'Needed to?'

She shrugged, her teeth gnawing on her bottom teeth. 'I haven't got to the bottom of that yet, but…'

She gazed up at him, her hazel eyes steady and resolute, her chin at an angle, as if daring him to challenge her.

'I didn't have the heart to refuse him.'

'The same way you're hoping I won't refuse Elsie.'

'That's between you and her.'

'Don't you hold even the slightest grudge, Meg?'

'Don't you think it's time you let yours go?'

He swung away. Brilliant. Not only did she think him financially unsound, but she thought him irresponsible and immature on top of it.

At least he could answer one of those charges. 'Early in my working life I set up a financial security blanket, so to speak.' He'd invested in real estate. Quite a bit of it, actually.

Her eyes widened. 'You did?'

He had to grit his teeth at her incredulity. 'Yes.'

She pursed her lips and stared at him as if she'd never seen him before. 'That was very sensible of you.'

He ground his teeth harder. He'd watched Laurie Parrish for many years and, while he might not like the man, had learned a thing or two that he'd put into practice. Those wise investments had paid off.

'I have enough money to tide me over for the next six weeks.' And beyond. But he resisted the impulse to brag and tell her exactly how much money that financial security blanket of his held—that really would be immature.

'Okay.' She eyed him uncertainly. 'Good. I'm glad that's settled.'

'While we're on the subject of personal questions—' he rounded on her '—you want to tell me what you're trying to achieve with this godforsaken wedding?'

She hitched up her chin and stuck out a hip. 'I'm joying this "godforsaken wedding" up,' she told him. 'I'm going to *force* them to celebrate.'

He gaped at her. 'Why?'

'Because there was no joy when we were growing up.'

'They were never there for us, Meg. They don't deserve this—the effort you put in, the—'

'Everyone deserves the right to a little happiness. And if they truly want to mend bridges, then...'

'Then?'

'Then I only think it fair and right that we give them that opportunity.'

Ben's face closed up. Every single time he came home Meg cursed what his mother had done to him—abandoning him like she had with a woman who'd grown old before her time. Usually she would let a topic like this drop. Today she didn't.

If Ben truly wanted to be a father, he needed to deal with his past.

She folded her arms, her heart pounding against the walls of her chest. 'When my mother died, my father just shut down, became a shell. Her death—it broke him. There was no room in his life for joy or celebration.'

Ben pushed his face in close to hers, his eyes flashing. 'He should've made an effort for you.'

Meg's hand slid across her stomach. She'd make every effort for *her* child, she couldn't imagine ever emotionally abandoning it, but maybe men were different—especially men of her father's generation.

She glanced at Ben. If a woman ever broke his heart, how would he react? She bit back a snigger. To break his heart a woman would have to get close to Ben, and he was never going to let that happen.

Ben's gaze lowered to where her hand rested against her stomach. His gaze had kept returning to her baby bump all morning. As if he couldn't get his fill. She swallowed. It was disconcerting, being the subject of his focus.

Not her, she corrected, the baby.

That didn't prevent the heat from rising in her

cheeks or her breathing from becoming shallow and strained.

She tried to shake herself free from whatever weird and wacky pregnancy hormone currently gripped her. *Concentrate.*

'So,' she started, 'while my father went missing in action, your mother left you with Elsie and disappeared. She never rang or sent a letter or anything. Elsie must've been worried sick. She must've been afraid to love you.'

He snapped back. 'Afraid to—?'

'I mean, what if your mother came back and took you away and she never heard from either of you again? What if, when you grew up, you did exactly what your mother did and abandoned *her*?'

'My mother abandoned me, not Elsie.'

'She abandoned the both of you, Ben.'

His jaw dropped open.

Meg nodded. 'Yes, you're right. They both should've made a bigger effort for us. But at least we found each other. At least we both had one friend in the world we could totally depend upon. And whatever else you want to dispute, you can't deny that we didn't have fun together.'

He rolled his shoulders. 'I don't want to deny that.'

'Well, can't you see that my father and Elsie didn't even have that much? Life has left them crippled. But...' She swallowed. 'I demand joy in my life now, and I won't compromise on that. If they refuse to get into the swing of this wedding then I'll know those bridges—the distance between us—can never be mended. And I'll have my answer.'

She hauled in a breath. 'One last chance, Ben, that was what I'm giving them.' And that's what she wanted him to give them too.

Ben didn't say anything. She cast a sidelong glance at him and bit back a sigh. She wondered when Ben—*her* Ben, the Ben she knew, the Ben with an easy smile and a careless saunter, without a care in the world—would return. Ever since he'd pulled his bike to a halt out at the front of her house yesterday there'd been trouble in his eyes.

He turned to her, hands on hips. He had lean hips and a tall, rangy frame. With his blond-tipped hair he looked like a god. No wonder women fell for him left, right and centre.

Though if he'd had a little less in the charm and looks department maybe he'd have learned to treat those women with more sensitivity.

Then she considered his mother and thought maybe not.

'When was the last time *you* felt joyful?' she asked on impulse.

He scratched his chin. He still hadn't shaved. He should look scruffy, but the texture of his shadowed jaw spoke to some yearning deep inside her. The tips of her fingers tingled. She opened and closed her hands. If she reached out and—

She shook herself. Ben *did* look scruffy. Completely and utterly. He most certainly didn't look temptingly disreputable with all that bad-boy promise of his.

Her hands continued to open and close. She heaved back a sigh. Okay, we'll maybe he did. But that certainly wasn't the look she was into.

Normally.

She scowled. Darn pregnancy hormones. And then the memory of that long ago kiss hit her and all the hairs on her arms stood to attention.

Stop it! She and Ben would never travel down that road again. There was simply too much at stake to risk it. *Ever.*

She folded her arms and swallowed. 'It can't be that hard, can it?' she demanded when he remained silent. Ben was the last person who'd need lessons in joy, surely?

'There are just so many to choose from,' he drawled, with that lazy hit-you-in-the-knees grin.

The grin was too slow coming to make her heart beat faster. Her heart had already started to sink. Ben was lying and it knocked her sideways. She'd always thought his exciting, devil-may-care life of freedom gave him endless pleasure and joy.

'The most recent instance that comes to mind is when I bungee-jumped over the Zambezi River from the Victoria Falls Bridge. Amazing rush of adrenaline. I felt like a superhero.'

She scratched a hand back through her hair. What was she thinking? Of *course* Ben's life gave him pleasure. He did so many exciting things. Did he really think he could give that all up for bottles and nappies?

'What about you? When was the last time you felt joyful?'

She didn't even need to think. She placed a hand across her stomach. And even amid all her current confusion and, yes, fear a shaft of joy lifted her up. She smiled. 'The moment I found out I was pregnant.'

She was going to have a baby!

'And every single day after, just knowing I'm pregnant.' Ben had made that possible. She would never be able to thank him enough. Ever.

She set her shoulders. When he came to the conclusion she knew he would—that he wasn't cut out for domesticity—she would do everything in her power to make sure he felt neither guilty nor miserable about it.

Ben shaded his eyes and stared out at the perfect crescent of the bay. 'So you want to spread the joy, huh?'

'Absolutely.' Being pregnant had changed her perspective. In comparison to so many other people she was lucky. Very lucky. 'We know how to do joy, Ben, but my father and Elsie—well, they've either forgotten how or they never knew the secret in the first place.'

'It's not a secret, Meg.'

Tell her father and Elsie that.

'And if this scheme of yours doesn't work and they remain as sour and distant as ever?'

'I'm not going to break my heart over it, if that's what you're worried about. But at least I'll know I tried.'

He shifted his weight and shoved his hands into the pockets of his jeans, making them ride even lower on his hips. The scent of leather slugged her in the stomach—which was odd, because Ben wasn't wearing his leather jacket.

'And what if it does work? Have you considered that?'

She dragged her gaze from his hips and tried to focus. 'That scenario could be the most challenging of all,' she agreed. 'The four of us...five,' she amended, glancing down at her stomach, 'all trying to become a family after all this time. It'll be tricky.'

She wanted to add, *but not impossible*, but her throat had closed over at the way he surveyed her stomach. Her chest tightened at the intensity of his focus. The light in his eyes made her thighs shake.

She cleared her throat and dragged in a breath. 'If it works I'll get a warm and fuzzy feeling,' she declared. Warm and fuzzy was preferable to hot and prickly. She rolled her shoulders. 'And perhaps you will too.'

Finally—*finally*—his gaze lifted to hers. 'More fairytales, Meg?'

Did he still hold that much resentment about their less than ideal childhood? 'You still want to punish them?'

'No.' Very slowly he shook his head. 'But I don't

think they deserve all your good efforts either. Especially when I'm far from convinced anything either one of us does will make a difference where they're concerned.'

'But what is it going to hurt to try?'

'I'm afraid it'll hurt *you.*'

He'd always looked out for her. She couldn't help but smile at him. 'I have a baby on the way. I'm on top of the world.'

He smiled suddenly too. A real smile—not one to trick or beguile. 'All right, Meg, I'm in. I'll do whatever I can to help.'

She let out a breath she hadn't even known she'd held.

'On one condition.'

She should've known. She folded her arms. 'Which is…?' She was *not* letting him sleep in her spare bedroom. He belonged next door. Besides… She swallowed. She needed her own space.

'You'll let me touch the baby.'

CHAPTER FIVE

MEG COULDN'T HELP her sudden grin. Lots of people had touched her baby bump—happy for her and awed by the miracle growing inside her. Why should Ben be any different?

Of course he'd be curious.

Of course he'd be invested.

He might never be Daddy but he'd always be Uncle Ben. *Favourite* Uncle Ben. Wanting to touch her baby bump was the most natural thing in the world.

She didn't try to temper her grin. 'Of course you can, Ben.'

She turned so she faced him front-on, offering her stomach to him, so to speak. His hands reached out, both of them strong and sure. They didn't waver. His hands curved around her abdomen—and just like that it stopped being the most natural thing in the world.

The pulse jammed in Meg's throat and she had to fight the urge to jolt away from him. Ben's hands suddenly didn't look like the hands of her best friend. They looked sensual and sure and knowing. They didn't feel like the hands of her best friend either.

Her breath hitched and her pulse skipped and spun like a kite-surfer in gale force winds. With excruciating thoroughness he explored every inch of her stomach through the thin cotton of her shirt. His fingers were hot and strong and surprisingly gentle.

And every part of her he touched he flooded with warmth and vigour.

She clenched her eyes shut. Her *best friend* had never looked at her with that possessive light in his eyes before. Not that it was aimed at her per se. Still, the baby was inside *her* abdomen.

He moved in closer and his heat swamped her. She opened her eyes and tried to focus on the quality of the light hitting the water of the bay below. But then his scent swirled around her—a mix of soap and leather and something darker and more illicit, like a fine Scotch whisky. She dragged in a shaky breath. Scotch wasn't Ben's drink. It was a crazy association. That thought, though, didn't make the scent go away.

Her heart all but stopped when he knelt down

in front of her and pressed the left side of his face to her stomach, his arm going about her waist. She found her hand hovering above his head. She wanted to rest it there, but that would make them seem too much of a trio. Her throat thickened and tears stung her eyes. They weren't a trio. Even if by some miracle Ben stayed, they still wouldn't be a trio.

But he wouldn't stay.

And so her hand continued to hover awkwardly above his head.

'Hey, little baby,' he crooned. 'I'm your—'

'No!' She tried to move away but his grip about her tightened.

'I'm…I'm pleased to meet you,' he whispered against her stomach instead.

She closed her eyes and breathed hard.

When he climbed back to his feet their gazes clashed and locked. She'd never felt more confused in her entire life.

'Thank you.'

'You're welcome.'

Their gazes continued to battle until Ben finally took a step away and seemed to mentally shake himself. 'What's the plan for the rest of the day?'

The plan was to put as much distance between

her and Ben as she could. Somewhere in the last day he'd become a stranger to her. A stranger who smelled good, who looked good, and who unnerved her.

This new Ben threatened more than her equilibrium. He threatened her unborn child's future and its happiness.

The Ben she knew would never do anything to hurt her. But this new Ben? She didn't trust him. She wanted to be away from him, to get her head back into some semblance of working order. She knew exactly how to accomplish that.

'I'm going into Nelson Bay to start on the wedding preparations.'

'Excellent plan. I'll come with you.'

She nearly choked. 'You'll what?'

'You said you wanted my help.' He lifted his arms. 'I'm yours to command.'

Why did that have to sound so suggestive?

'But—' She tried to think of something sensible to say. She couldn't, so she strode back around the side of the house.

'Time is a-wasting.' He kept perfect time beside her.

'It's really not necessary.' She tucked her hair back behind her ears, avoiding eye contact while she collected the tape measure along with the measurements he'd jotted down for her. 'You only got back from Africa yesterday. You are allowed a couple of days to catch your breath.'

'Are you trying to blow me off, Meg?'

Heat scorched her cheeks. 'Of course not.'

He grinned as if enjoying her discomfiture. 'Well, then…'

She blew out a breath. 'Have it your own way. But we're taking my car, not the bike, and I'm driving.'

'Whatever you say.'

He raised his hands in mock surrender, and suddenly he was her Ben again and it made her laugh. 'Be warned—I *will* make you buy me an ice cream cone. I cannot get enough of passionfruit ripple ice cream at the moment.'

He glanced at his watch. 'It's nearly lunchtime. I'll buy you a kilo of prawns from the co-op and we can stretch out on the beach and eat them.'

'You'll have to eat them on your own, then. And knowing how I feel about prawns, that'd be too cruel.'

He followed her into the house. 'They give you morning sickness?'

She patted her stomach. 'It has something to do

with mercury levels in seafood. It could harm the baby. I'm afraid Camembert and salami are off the menu too.'

He stared at her, his jaw slack, and she could practically read his thoughts—shock that certain foods might harm the baby growing inside her— and his sudden confrontation with his own ignorance. Her natural impulse was to reassure him, but she stifled it. Ben was ignorant about babies and pregnancy, and it wasn't up to her to educate him. If he wanted to be a good father he would have to educate himself, exercising his own initiative, not because she prompted or nagged him to.

But she didn't want the stranger back, so she kept her voice light and added, 'Not to mention wine and coffee. All of my favourite things. Still, I seem to be finding ample consolation in passion-fruit ripple ice cream.'

She washed her hands, dried them, stowed the measurements in her handbag and then lifted an eyebrow in Ben's direction. 'Ready?'

He still hadn't moved from his spot in the doorway, but at her words he strode across to the sink to pump the strawberry-scented hand-wash she kept on the window ledge into his hands. The scent only seemed to emphasise his masculinity. She watched him wash his hands and remembered the feel of them on her abdomen, their heat and their gentleness.

She jerked her gaze away.

'Ready.'

When she turned back he was drying his hands. And there was a new light in his eyes and a determined shape to his mouth. Normally she would take the time to dust a little powder on her nose and slick on a coat of lipstick, but she wanted to be out of the house and into the day. Right now!

She led the way to her car.

'Okay, the plan today is to hire a marquee for the big event—along with the associated paraphernalia. Tables chairs and whatnot,' she said as they drove the short distance to the neighbouring town. 'And then we'll reward ourselves with lunch.'

'Do you mind if we do a bit of shopping afterwards? I need to grab a few things.'

She glanced at him. Ben and shopping? She shook her head. 'Not at all.'

To Meg's utter surprise, Ben was a major help on the Great Marquee Hunt. He zeroed in immediately on the marquee that would best suit their purposes. The side panels could be rolled up to allow a breeze to filter through the interior if the evening proved warm. If the day was cool, however—and that wasn't unheard of in late March—the view of the bay could still be enjoyed through the clear panels that acted like windows in the marquee walls.

Ben insisted on putting down the deposit himself.

Given the expression on his face earlier, when she'd asked him about his financial circumstances, she decided it would be the better part of valour not to argue with him.

Furniture was next on the list, and Meg chose round tables and padded chairs. 'Round tables means the entire table can talk together with ease.' Hopefully it would promote conversation.

Ben's lips twisted. 'And they'll make the marquee look fuller, right?'

Exactly.

'What else?' he demanded.

'We need a long table for the wedding party.'

'There's only four of us. It won't need to be *that* long.'

'And tables for presents and the cake.'

Ben pointed out tables, the salesman made

a note, and then they were done—all in under an hour.

Ben's hands went to his hips. 'What now?'

To see him so fully focused on the task made her smile. 'Now we congratulate ourselves on having made such excellent progress and reward ourselves with lunch.'

'That's it?'

She could tell he didn't believe her. 'It's one of the big things ticked off. It's all I had scheduled for today.'

'What are the other big things?'

'The catering, the cake, the invitations. And...' A grin tugged at her lips.

He leaned down to survey her face. His own lips twitched. 'And?'

'And shopping for Elsie's outfit.'

He shot away from her. 'Oh, no—no, no. You're *not* dragging me along on that.'

She choked back a laugh. 'Fat lot of use you'd be anyway. I'll let you off the hook if you buy me lunch.'

'Deal.'

They bought hot chips smothered in salt and vinegar, and dashed across the road to the beach. School had gone back several weeks ago, but it was the weekend and the weather was divine. The long crescent of sand that bordered the bay was lined with families enjoying the sunshine, sand and water. Children's laughter, the sounds of waves whooshing up onto the beach and the cries of seagulls greeted them. *Divine!* She lifted her face to the sun and breathed it all in.

They found a spare patch of sand and Meg stretched out her legs, relishing the warmth of the sun on the bare skin of her arms and legs. She glanced at Ben as he hunkered down beside her. He must be hot.

'You should've changed into shorts.'

He unwrapped the chips. 'I'm good.'

Yeah, but he'd look great in shorts, and—

She blinked. What on earth…? And then the scent of salt and vinegar hit her and her stomach grumbled and her mouth watered. With a grin he held the packet towards her.

They ate, not saying much, just listening to the familiar sounds of children at play and the splashing of the tiny waves that broke onshore. Nearby a moored yacht's rigging clanged in the breeze, making a pelican lift out of the water and wheel up into the air. It was summer in the bay—her favourite time of year and her favourite patch of paradise.

She wasn't sure when they both started to observe the family—just that at some stage the nearby mother, father and two small girls snagged their attention. One of the little girls dashed down the beach towards them, screaming with delight when her father chased after her. Seizing her securely around the waist, he lifted her off her feet to swing her above his head.

'Higher, Daddy, higher!' she squealed, laughing down at him, her face alive with delight.

The other little girl, smaller than the first, lurched across the sand on chubby, unsteady legs to fling her arms around her father's thigh. She grinned and chortled up at him.

Meg swallowed and her chest started to cramp. Both of those little girls literally glowed with their love for their father.

She tore her gaze away to stare directly out in front of her, letting the sunlight that glinted off the water to dazzle and half-blind her.

'More?' Ben's voice came out hoarse and strained as he held the chips out to her.

She shook her head. Her appetite had fled.

He scrunched the remaining chips and she was aware of every crackle the paper made. And how white his knuckles had turned. She went back to staring directly out in front of her, tracking a speedboat as it zoomed past.

But it didn't drown out the laughter of the two little girls.

'Did you ever consider what you were depriving your child of when you decided to go it alone, Meg?'

His voice exploded at her—tight and barely controlled. She stiffened. And then she rounded on him. 'Don't take that high moral tone with me, Ben Sullivan! Since when in your entire adult life, have you *ever* put another person's needs or wants above your own?'

He blinked. 'I—'

'I didn't twist your arm. You had some say in the matter, you know.'

Her venom took him off guard. It took her off guard too, but his question had sliced right into the core of her. She'd thought she'd considered that question. She'd thought it wouldn't matter. But after seeing that family—the girls with their father, their love and sense of belonging—she felt the doubt demons rise to plague her.

'Families come in all shapes and sizes,' she hissed, more for her own benefit than his. Her baby would want for nothing! 'As for depriving my child of a father? Well, I don't rate my father very highly, and I sure as heck don't rate yours. There are worse things than not having a father.'

Ben's head rocked back in shock. Meg's sentiment didn't surprise him, but the way she expressed it did.

He clenched his jaw so hard he thought he might break teeth. A weight pressed against his chest, making it difficult to breathe.

'Just like you don't rate me as a father, right?' he rasped out, acid burning his throat.

Eventually he turned to look at her. She immediately glanced away, but not before he recognised the scepticism stretching through her eyes. The weight in his chest grew heavier. If Meg didn't have any faith in him…

No, dammit! He clenched his hands. Meg didn't have all the answers.

He swore.

She flinched.

He kept his voice low. 'So I'm suitable as a sperm bank but not as anything more substantial?' Was *that* how she saw him?

She stared straight back out in front of her. 'That surprises you?'

'It does when that's your attitude, Meg.'

That made her turn to look at him.

Dammit it all to hell, she was supposed to *know* him!

A storm raged in the hazel depths of her eyes. He watched her swallow. She glanced down at her hands and then back up. 'How long have you wanted to be a father, Ben? A week?'

It was his turn to glance away.

'I've wanted to be a mother for as long as I can remember.'

'And you think that gives you more rights?'

'It means I know what to expect. It means I know I'm not going to change my mind next week. It means I know I'm committed to this child.' She slapped a hand to the sand. 'It means I know precisely what I'm getting into—that I've put plans into place in anticipation of the baby's arrival, and that I've adjusted my life so I can ensure my baby gets the very best care and has the very best life I can possibly give it. And now you turn up and think you have the right to tell me I'm selfish!'

She let out a harsh laugh that had his stomach churning.

'When have you ever committed to anybody or anything? You've never even taken a job on full-time. You've certainly never committed to a woman or what's left of your family. It's barely possible to get you to commit to dinner at the end of next week!'

'I'm committed to *you*.' The words burst out of him. 'If you'd ever needed me, Meg, I'd have come home.'

She smiled then, but there was an ache of sadness behind her eyes that he didn't understand. 'Yes, I believe you would've. But once I was back on my feet you'd have been off like a flash again, wouldn't you?'

He had no answer to that.

'The thing is, Ben, your trooping all over the world having adventures is fine in a best friend, but it's far from fine in a father.'

She had a point. He knew she did. And until he knew how involved he wanted to be he had no right to push her or judge her. 'I didn't mean to imply you were selfish. I think you'll be a great mum.'

But it didn't mean there wasn't room for him in the baby's life too.

She gestured to her right, to where that family now sat eating sandwiches, but she didn't look at them again. 'Is that what you really want?'

He stared at the picture of domestic bliss and

had to repress a shudder. He wasn't doing marriage. Ever. He didn't believe in it. But… The way those little girls looked at their father—their faces so open and trusting. And loving. The thought of having someone look up to him like that both terrified and electrified him.

If he wanted to be a father—a proper father—his life would have to change. Drastically.

'Ben, I want a better father for my child than either one of us had.'

'Me too.' That at least was a no-brainer.

She eyed him for a moment. Whenever she was in the sun for any length of time the green flecks within the brown of her iris grew in intensity. They flashed and sparkled now, complementing the aqua water only a few feet away.

Aqua eyes.

A smattering of freckles across her nose.

Blonde hair that brushed her shoulders.

And she smelled like pineapple and coconuts.

She was a golden goddess, encapsulating all he most loved about summer.

'Ben!'

He snapped to. 'What?'

Her nostrils flared, drawing his attention back to her freckles. She glanced away and then back again. 'I said, you *do* know that I'm not anti-commitment the way you are, right?'

'Yeah, sure.'

His attention remained on those cute freckles, their duskiness highlighting the golden glow of her skin. He'd never noticed how cute they were before—cute and kind of cheeky. They were new to him. This conversation wasn't. Commitment versus freedom. They'd thrashed it out endless time. To her credit, though, Meg had never tried to change his mind. They'd simply agreed to disagree. Even that one stupid time they had kissed.

Damn it! He'd promised never to think about that again.

'Then you should also be aware that I don't expect to *"deprive"*—' she made quotation marks in the air with her fingers '—my child of a father for ever.'

He frowned, still distracted by those freckles, and then by the shine on her lips when she moistened them. 'Right.'

She hauled in a breath and let it out again. The movement wafted a slug of coconut infused pineapple his way. He drew it into his lungs slowly, the way he would breathe in a finely aged Chardonnay before bringing the glass to his lips and sipping it.

'Just because I've decided to have a baby it doesn't mean I've given up on the idea of falling in love and getting married, maybe having more kids if I'm lucky.'

It took a moment for the significance of her words to connect, but when they did they smashed into him with the force of that imaginary bottle of Chardonnay wielded at his head. The beach tilted. The world turned black and white. He shoved his hands into the sand and clenched them.

'I might be doing things slightly out of order, but…' She let her words trail off.

He stabbed a finger at her, showering her with sand. 'You are *not* letting another man raise my child!'

He shot to his feet and paced down to the water's edge, tried to get his breathing back under control before he hyperventilated.

Another man would get the laughter…and the fun…and the love.

He dragged a hand back through his hair. Of course this schmuck would also be getting hog-tied into marriage and would have to deal with school runs, parent and teacher interviews and eat-your-greens arguments. But…

'No!'

He swung around to find Meg standing directly behind him. 'Keep your voice down,' she ordered, glancing around. 'There are small children about.'

Why the hell didn't she just bar him from all child-friendly zones? She obviously didn't rate his parenting abilities at all. His hands clenched. But giving his child—*his child*—to another man to raise? No way!

He must have said it out loud, because she arched an eyebrow at him. 'You think you can prevent me from marrying whoever I want?'

'Whomever,' he said, knowing that correcting her grammar would set her teeth on edge.

Which it did. 'You and whose army, Ben?'

'You can marry *whomever* you damn well please,' he growled, 'but this baby only has one father.' He pounded a fist to his chest. 'And that's me.'

She folded her arms. 'You're telling me that you're giving up your free and easy lifestyle to settle in Port Stephens, get a regular job and trade your motorbike for a station wagon?'

'That's exactly what I'm saying.'

'Why?'

It was a genuine question, not a challenge. He didn't know how to articulate the determination or sense of purpose that had overtaken him. He only knew that this decision was the most important of his life.

And he had no intention of getting it wrong.

He knew that walking away from their baby would be wrong.

But…

It left the rest of his life in tatters.

Meg sighed when he remained silent. She didn't believe he meant it. It was evident in her face, in her body language, in the way she turned away. Her lack of faith in him stung, but he had no one else to blame for that but himself.

He would prove himself to her. He would set all her fears to rest. And he would be the best father on the planet.

When she turned back he could see her nose had started to turn pink. Her nose always went pink before she cried. He stared at the pinkness. He glanced away. Meg hardly ever cried.

He glanced back. Swallowed. It could be sunburn. They'd been out in the sun for a while now.

He closed his eyes. He ached to wrap her in his arms and tell her he would not let either her or the baby down. Words, though, were cheap. Meg would need more than verbal assurances. She'd need action.

'We should make tracks.' She shaded her eyes against the sun. 'You said you needed to do some shopping?'

He did. But he needed a timeout from Meg more. He needed to get his head around the realisation that he was back in Port Stephens for good.

He feigned interest in a sultry brunette, wearing nothing but a bikini, who was ambling along the beach towards them.

'Ben?'

He lifted one shoulder in a lazy shrug. 'The shopping can wait.' He deliberately followed the brunette's progress instead of looking at Meg. 'Look, why don't you head off? I might hang around for a while. I'll find my own way home.'

He knew exactly what interpretation Meg would put on that.

The twist of her lips told her she had. Without another word, she turned and left.

Clenching his hands, he set off down the beach, not even noticing the brunette when he passed her.

A baby deserves to have the unconditional love of the two people who created it. If he left, who would his child have in its day-to-day life? Meg, who'd be wonderful, and Uncle Ben who'd never be there. His hands clenched. Meg's father and Elsie could hardly be relied on to provide the baby with emotional support.

He shook his head. He could at least make sure this child knew it was loved and wanted by its father. Things like that—they did matter.

And this baby deserved only good things.

When he reached the end of the beach he turned and walked back and then headed for the shops. Meg should be home by now, and he meant to buy every damn book about pregnancy and babies he could get his hands on. He wanted to be prepared for the baby's arrival. He wanted to help Meg out in any way he could.

What he didn't need was her damn superiority, or her looking over his shoulder and raising a sceptical eyebrow at the books he selected. He had enough doubt of his own to deal with.

He turned back to stare at the beach, the bay, and the water. Back in Port Stephens for good?

Him?

Hell.

CHAPTER SIX

MEG SANG ALONG to her Madonna CD in full voice. She'd turned the volume up loud to disguise the fact she couldn't reach the high notes and in an attempt to drown out the chorus of voices that plagued her—a litany of 'what ifs' and 'what the hells' and 'no ways'. All circular and pointless. But persistent. Singing helped to quiet them.

She broke off to complete a complicated manoeuvre with her crochet needle. At least as far as she was concerned it was complicated. Her friend Ally assured her that by the time she finished this baby shawl she'd have this particular stitch combination down pat.

She caressed the delicate white wool and surveyed her work so far. It didn't seem like much, considering how long it had taken her, but she didn't begrudge a moment of that time. She'd have this finished in time for the baby's arrival. Maybe only just, but it would be finished. And then she could wrap her baby in this lovely soft shawl, its wool so delicate it wouldn't irritate newborn skin. She'd wrap her baby in this shawl and it would know how much it was loved.

She lifted it to her cheek and savoured its softness.

The song came to an end. She lowered the crocheting back to her lap and was about to resume when some sixth sense had her glancing towards the doorway.

Ben.

Her throat tightened. She swallowed once, twice. 'Hey,' she finally managed.

'I knocked.' He pointed back behind him.

She grabbed the remote, turned the music down and motioned for him to take a seat. 'With the music blaring like that there's not a chance I'd have heard you.'

He stood awkwardly in the doorway. She gripped the crochet needle until the metal bit into her fingers.

'Madonna, huh?' He grinned but it didn't hide his discomfort.

'Yup.' She grinned back but she doubted it hid her tension, her uneasiness either.

He glanced around. 'We never sat in here when we were growing up.'

'No.' When they'd been growing up this had definitely been adult territory. When indoors, they'd stuck to the kitchen and the family room. 'But this is my house now and I can sit where I please.'

He didn't look convinced. Tension kept his spine straight and his shoulders tight. Last week she'd have risen and led him through to the family room, where he'd feel more comfortable. This week…?

She lifted her chin. This week making Ben comfortable was the last thing on her agenda. That knowledge made her stomach churn and bile rise in her throat. It didn't mean she wanted to make him *un*comfortable, though.

She cleared her throat. 'Have a look out of the front window.'

After a momentary hesitation he did as she ordered.

'It has the most divine view of the bay. I find that peaceful. When the wind is up you can hear the waves breaking on shore.'

'And that's a sound you've always loved.' He settled on the pristine white leather sofa. 'And you can hear it best in here.'

And in the front bedroom. She didn't mention that, though. Mentioning bedrooms to Ben didn't seem wise. Which was crazy. But…

She glanced at him and her pulse sped up and her skin prickled. *That* was what was crazy. He sprawled against the sofa with that easy, long-limbed grace of his, one arm resting along the back of the sofa as if in invitation. Her crochet needle trembled.

She dragged her gaze away and set her crochet work to one side. Her life was in turmoil. That was all this was—a reaction to all the changes happening in her life. The fact she had a baby on the way. The fact her father was marrying Elsie. The fact Ben claimed he wanted to be a father.

Ben nodded towards the wool. 'What are you doing?'

She had to moisten her lips before she could speak. 'I'm making a shawl for the baby.'

She laid the work out for him to see and he stared at it as if fascinated. When he glanced up at her, the warmth in those blue eyes caressed her.

'You can knit?'

She pretended to preen. 'Why, yes, I can, now that you mention it. Knitting clubs were more popular than book clubs around here for a while. But this isn't knitting—it's crochet, and I'm in the process of mastering the art.'

He frowned. And then he straightened. 'Why? Are you trying to save money?'

She folded her arms. That didn't deserve an answer.

His eyes narrowed. 'Or is this what your social life had descended to?'

If she could have kept a straight face she'd have let him go on believing that. It would be one seriously scary picture of life here in Fingal Bay for him to chew over. One he'd probably run from kicking and screaming. But she couldn't keep a straight face.

He leant back, his shoulders loosening, his grin hooking up one side of his face in that slow, melt-a-woman-to-her-core way he had. 'Okay, just call me an idiot.'

If she's had any breath left in her lungs she might have done exactly that. Only that grin of his had knocked all the spare oxygen out of her body.

'Your social life is obviously full. I've barely clapped eyes on you these last few days.'

Had he wanted to? The thought made her heart skip and stutter a little faster.

Stop being stupid! 'It's full enough for me.' She didn't tell him that Monday night had been an antenatal class, or that last night she'd cooked dinner for Ally, who was recovering from knee surgery. Ben's social life consisted of partying hard and having a good time, not preparing for babies or looking after friends.

Ben's life revolved around adrenaline junkie thrills, drinking hard and chasing women. She wondered why he wasn't out with that sexy brunette this evening—the one he'd obviously had every intention of playing kiss chase with the other day—and then kicked herself. Sunday to Wednesday? Ben would count that a long-term relationship. And they both knew what he thought about those.

'So why?' He gestured to the wool.

He really didn't get it, did he? An ache pressed behind her eyes. What the hell was he doing here? She closed her eyes, dragged in a breath and then opened them again. She settled more comfortably in her chair.

'Once upon a time...' she started.

Ben eased back in his seat too, slouching slightly, his eyes alive with interest.

'Once upon a time,' she repeated, 'the Queen announced she was going to have a baby. There was much rejoicing in the kingdom.'

He grinned that grin of his. 'Of course there was.'

'To celebrate and honour the impending arrival of the royal heir, the Queen fashioned a special shawl for the child to be wrapped in. It took an entire nine months to make, and every stitch was a marvel of delicate skill, awe-inspiring craftsmanship and love. All who saw it bowed down in awe.'

He snorted. 'Laying it on a bit thick, Meg. A shawl is never going to be a holy grail.'

She tossed her head. 'All who saw it bowed down in awe, recognising it as the symbol of maternal love that it was.'

The teasing in Ben's face vanished. He stared at her with an intensity that made her swallow.

'When the last stitch was finished, the Queen promptly gave birth. And it was said that whenever the royal child was wrapped in that shawl its crying stopped and it was immediately comforted.' She lifted her chin. 'The shawl became a valued family heirloom, passed down throughout the generations.'

He eyed the work spread in her lap. Was it her imagination or did he fully check her chest out on the way down? Her pulse pounded. Wind rushed in her ears.

'You want to give your baby something special.'

His words pulled her back from her ridiculous

imaginings. 'Yes.' She wanted to fill her baby's life with love and all manner of special things. The one thing she didn't want to give it was a father who would let it down. She didn't say that out loud, though. Ben knew her feelings on the subject. Harping on it would only get his back up. He had to come to the conclusion that he wasn't father material in his own time.

She didn't want to talk about the baby with Ben any longer. She didn't have the heart for it.

'So, how's your week been so far?'

His lips twisted. 'How the hell do you deal with Elsie?'

Ah.

'The woman is a goddamn clam—a locked box. I'm never going to get those names for you Meg.'

She'd known it would be a tough test. But if Ben couldn't pass it he had no business hanging around in Fingal Bay.

His eyes flashed. 'Is it against the rules to help me out?'

She guessed not. He'd still have to do the hard work, but...

She didn't want to help him. She stared down at her hands. She wanted him to leave Fingal Bay and not come back for seven, eight...ten months.

He's your best friend!

And he was turning her whole life upside down. Not to mention her baby's.

She remembered the way she'd ached for her father to show some interest in her life, to be there for her. And she remembered the soul-deep disappointment, the crushing emptiness, the disillusionment and the shame when he'd continued to turn away from her. Nausea swirled in her stomach. She didn't want that for her child.

Did her baby need protecting from Ben? She closed her eyes. If she knew the answer to that…

'Why didn't you come over for dinner tonight? Elsie says you come to dinner every Wednesday night.'

She opened her eyes to find him leaning towards her. She shrugged. 'Except when you're home.'

His lips, which were normally relaxed and full of wicked promise, pressed into a thin line. 'And why's that?'

'I like to give you guys some space when you're home.'

'Is that all?'

Her automatic response was to open her mouth to tell him of course that was all. She stamped on it. Ben had changed everything when he'd burst in on Saturday. She wasn't sure she wanted to shield him any more. 'Precisely how much honesty do you want, Ben?'

His jaw slackened. 'I thought we were always honest.'

She pursed her lips. 'I'm about as honest as I can be when I see you for a total of three weeks in a year. Four if I'm lucky.'

His jaw clenched. His nostrils flared. 'Why didn't you come over to Elsie's tonight?'

Fine. She folded her arms. 'There are a couple of reasons. The first: Elsie is hard work. You're home so you can deal with her. It's nice to have a night off.'

He sagged back as if she'd slugged him on the jaw.

'I make her cook dinner for me every Wednesday night. It's a bargain we struck up. I do her groceries and she cooks me dinner on Wednesday nights. But really it's so I can make sure she's still functioning—keep an eye on her fine motor skills and whatnot. See if I can pick up any early signs of illness or dementia.'

Which proved difficult as Elsie had absolutely no conversation in her. Until one night about a month ago, when Elsie had suddenly started chatting and

Meg had fled. It shamed her now—her panic and sense of resentment and her cowardice. She could see now that Elsie had tried to open a door, and Meg had slammed it shut in her face.

Ben stared at her. He didn't say a word. It was probably why Elsie had reverted to being a clam around Ben now.

Still, it wasn't beyond Ben to make an overture too, was it? Meg bit her lip. If he truly wanted to be a father.

'Look, when you breeze in for an odd week here and a few days there, I do my best to make it fun and not to bore you with tedious domestic details. But if you mean to move back to Port Stephens for good then you can jolly well share some of the load.'

He'd gone pale, as if he might throw up on her pristine white carpet. 'What's the other reason you didn't come to dinner?' he finally asked.

She swallowed. Carpets could be cleaned. It was much harder to mend a child's broken heart. But...

'Meg?'

She lifted her chin and met his gaze head-on. 'I don't like seeing you and Elsie together. It's when I like you both least.'

He stared at her, his eyes dark. In one swift movement he rose. 'I should go.'

'Sit down, Ben.' She bit back a sigh. 'Do you mean to run away every time we have a difficult conversation? What about if that difficult conversation is about the baby? Are you going to run away then too?'

The pulse at the base of his jaw pounded. 'Couldn't you at least offer a guy a beer before tearing his character to shreds?'

She stood. 'You're right. But not a beer. You drink too much.'

'Hell, Meg, don't hold back!'

She managed a smile. Somehow. 'I'm having a hot chocolate. I'm trying to make sure I get enough calcium. Would you like one too, or would you prefer tea or coffee?'

He didn't answer, and she led the way to the kitchen and set about making hot chocolate. She was aware of how closely Ben watched her—she'd have had to be blind not to. It should have made her clumsy, but it didn't. It made her feel powerful and…and beautiful.

Which didn't make sense.

She shook the thought off and handed Ben one of the steaming mugs. 'Besides,' she started, as if there hadn't been a long, silent pause in their conversation, 'I'm not shredding your character. You're my best friend and I love you.'

She pulled a stool out at the breakfast bar and sat. 'But c'mon, Ben, what's to like about hanging out with you and Elsie? She barely speaks and you turn back into a sullen ten-year-old. All the conversation is left to me. You don't help me out, and Elsie answers any questions directed to her in words of two syllables. Preferably one if she can get away with it. Great night out for a girl.' She said it all with a grin, wanting to chase the shadows from his eyes.

'I...' Ben slammed his mug down, pulled out the stool beside her and wrapped an arm about her shoulders in a rough hug. 'Hell, Meg, I'm sorry. I never looked at it that way before.'

'That's okay.' He smelled of leather and Scotch and her senses greedily drank him in. 'I didn't mind when your visits were so fleeting—they were like moments stolen from reality. They never seemed part of the real world.'

'Which will change if I become a permanent fixture in the area?'

Exactly. She reached for her mug again. Ben removed his arm. Even though it was a warm night she missed its weight and its strength.

'I deal with Elsie by telling her stories.'

He swung around so quickly he almost spilled his drink. 'Like our fairytales?'

She shook her head. No, not like those. They were just for her and Ben. 'I talk at her—telling her what I've been up to for the week, what child did what to another child at work, what I saw some-one wearing on the boardwalk in Nelson Bay, what wonderful new dish I've recently tried cooking, what book I'm reading. Just…monologues.'

It should be a tedious, monotonous rendition—a chore—but in between enquiring if Elsie had won anything at Housie or the raffles and if she'd made her shopping list yet, to amuse herself Meg dramatised everything to the nth degree. It made the time pass more quickly.

'So I should tell her what I've been up to?'

She shrugged.

'But I haven't been doing anything since I got back.'

She made her voice tart. 'Then I suggest you start doing something before you turn into a veg-etable.'

A laugh shot out of him. 'Like I said earlier, don't hold back.'

She had no intention of doing so, but… She glanced at the handsome profile beside her and an icy hand clamped around her heart and squeezed. Her chest constricted painfully. She didn't want to make Ben miserable. She didn't want him feeling bad about himself. She wanted him to be happy.

And living in Fingal Bay would never make him happy.

She dragged her gaze back to the mug she cradled in her hands. 'I already have the names of ten guests from my father.'

'How'd you manage that?'

'Deceit and emotional blackmail.'

He grinned. And then he threw his head back and laughed. Captured in the moment like that he looked so alive it momentarily robbed her of breath, of speech, and of coherent thought. She never felt so alive as when Ben was home. Yearning rose inside her. Yearning for…

He glanced at her, stilled, and his eyes darkened. It seemed as if the very air between them shimmered. They swayed towards each other.

And then they both snapped away. Meg grabbed their now empty mugs and bolted for the sink, desperately working on getting her breathing back under control. They'd promised one another that they would never go *there* again. They'd agreed their friendship was too important to risk. And that still held true.

In the reflection of the window she could see Ben pacing on the other side of the breakfast bar, his hands clenched. Eventually she wouldn't be able to pretend to be washing the cups any more.

Ben coughed and then stared up at the ceiling. 'Deceit and emotional blackmail?'

She closed her eyes, counted to three and turned off the tap. She turned back to him, praying—very hard—that she looked casual and unconcerned. 'I told him that Elsie would love a small party for a reception and that if he cared about Elsie's needs then he'd give me the names of ten people I could invite to the wedding.'

'It obviously worked.'

Like a charm. Her father and Elsie might not be particularly demonstrative, but Meg didn't doubt they cared deeply for each other. She remembered their linked hands, the fire in Elsie's eyes when she'd defended Laurie to Ben, and her father's vulnerability.

She glanced at Ben. He seemed completely unfazed by that 'moment'. The hot chocolate in her stomach curdled. Maybe she'd been the only one caught up in it.

She cleared her throat. 'It worked so well he actually gave me a dozen names.'

Ben rubbed his chin. 'If I did it in reverse…'

'Worth a try,' she agreed.

'Brilliant!' He slapped a hand down on the breakfast bar. 'Thanks, Meg.'

'Any time.'

But the words sounded wooden, even to her own ears. He opened the back door, hesitated, and then turned back. 'I didn't come back to make your life chaotic on purpose, Meg.'

She managed a smile. 'I know.'

'What night do you check up on your father?'

She should have known he'd make that connection. 'Tomorrow night. He refuses to cook, or to let me cook, so we have dinner at the RSL club.'

'Would it be all right if Elsie and I came along with you tomorrow night?'

What? Like a family? She frowned and scratched the back of her neck. Eventually she managed to clear her throat again. 'The more the merrier.'

'What time should we be ready?'

'He likes to eat early these days, so I'll be leaving here at six.'

With a nod, he was gone.

Ben stood in the dark garden, adrift between Meg's house and Elsie's.

He'd wandered over to Meg's tonight because he couldn't have stood another ten minutes in Elsie's company, but…

He scratched a hand back through his hair. He hadn't expected to be confronted with his own inadequacies. With his selfishness.

He threw his head back to glare at the stars. He dragged cleansing breaths into his lungs. No wonder Meg didn't believe he'd see this fatherhood gig through.

He rested his hands against his knees and swore. He had to start pulling his weight. Meg was pregnant. She should be focussing on things like getting ready for the baby. Resting.

While he'd been off seeing the world Meg had been taking care of everyone. He straightened. Well, her days of being a drudge were over. He'd see to that.

He glanced at his grandmother's house. Shoving his shoulders back, he set off towards it.

He found Elsie at the kitchen table, playing Soli-taire—just as she'd been doing when he'd left. The radio crooned songs from the 1950s.

'Drink?' he offered, going to the fridge.

'No, thank you.'

She didn't so much as glance at him. He grabbed a beer…stopped…set it back down again and seized a can of soda instead. The silence pressed down like a blanket of cold snow. He shot a glance towards the living room and the promised distrac-tion of the television.

You turn back into a sullen ten-year-old.

He pulled out a chair and sat at the table with Elsie—something he hadn't done since he'd re-turned home—and watched as she finished her game. She glanced at him and then in the wink of an eye, almost as if she were afraid he'd change his mind, she dealt them both out seven cards each.

'Can you play rummy?'

'Sure I can.'

'Laurie taught me.'

His skin tightened. He rolled his shoulders. So far this was the longest conversation they'd had all week. 'I…uh…when he was recuperating and you visited?'

'That's right.'

He wanted to get up from the table and flee. It all felt so wrong. But he remembered Meg's crack about him reverting to a sullen ten-year-old and swallowed. 'When I was in Alaska I played a form of rummy with the guys off the fishing trawlers. Those guys were ruthless.'

But Elsie, it seemed, had clammed up again, and Ben wondered if it was something he'd said.

They played cards for a bit. Finally he broke the silence. 'Meg's looking great. Pregnancy obviously agrees with her.'

Nothing.

'She's crocheting this thing—a baby shawl, I think she said. Looks hard, and progress is looking slow.' He picked up the three of spades Elsie had discarded. She still didn't say anything. He ground back a sigh. 'Can you crochet?'

'Yep.'

She could? He stared at her for a moment, trying not to rock back on his chair. 'You should ask her to bring this shawl over to show you. In fact, you should make something for the baby too.'

She didn't look up from her cards. 'Me?'

He frowned. 'And so should I.'

'You?' A snort accompanied the single syllable.

He cracked his knuckles. 'I might not be able to

knit or sew, but travelling in the remote parts of the world forces a guy to become pretty handy.'

Handy? *Ha!* He could fashion a makeshift compass, build a temporary shelter and sterilise water, but what on earth could he make for the baby that would be useful? And beautiful. Because he'd want it to be beautiful too. An heirloom.

'A crib.' As the idea occurred to him he said it out loud. He knew a bit about carpentry. 'I'll build a crib for the baby.' He laid out his trio of threes, a trio of jacks and placed his final card on Elsie's sevens. 'Gin.'

Elsie threw her cards down with a sniff.

'Best of three,' Ben announced. 'You're rusty. You need the practice. Though it's got to be said those Alaskan fisherman took no prisoners.'

Elsie picked up her second hand without a word. Ben mentally rolled his eyes. Meg was right. This was hard work. But he found a certain grim enjoyment in needling Elsie too.

As they played he found himself taking note of Elsie's movements. Her hands were steady and she held herself stiffly erect. No signs of a debilitating disease there as far as he could see. When she won the game in three moves he had to conclude that, while she didn't say much, her mind was razor-sharp.

'Gin!' There was no mistaking her triumph, but she still didn't crack a smile.

He snorted. 'I went easy on you.'

Her chin came up a notch. Her eyes narrowed.

'Oh, and by the way, we're having dinner with Meg and her father tomorrow evening at the club. I said we'd be ready at six.'

'Right.'

They played in silence for several moments, and then all in a rush it suddenly occurred to Ben that he might be cramping the older couple's style. He cleared his throat. It wasn't easy imagining Elsie and Mr Parrish wanting—needing—privacy. But that didn't change the fact that they were engaged.

'Do you mind me staying here while I'm in town?'

'No.'

'Look, if it's not convenient I can arrange alternative accommodation. I might be staying a bit longer than usual.'

'How long?'

'I'm not sure yet.'

Oh, he was sure, all right. He was staying for good. Meg should be the first to know that, though.

'I'd certainly understand it if you'd like me to find somewhere else to stay.'

'No.'

He stared at her. She didn't say any more. 'Did my mother really never contact you, not even once, after she left me here?'

The question shocked him as much as it probably shocked Elsie. He hadn't known it had been hovering on his lips, waiting to pounce. He hadn't known he still even cared what the answer to the damn question might be.

Elsie folded her cards up as tight as her face and dropped them to the table. 'No.'

Without another word she rose and left the room.

'Goodnight, Ben,' he muttered under his breath. 'Goodnight, Elsie,' he forced himself to call out. 'Thanks for the card game.'

Ben and Elsie strolled across to Meg's the next evening at six on the dot. At least Ben strolled. Elsie never did anything quite so relaxed as stroll. Her gait was midway between a trudge and a march.

They waited while Meg reversed her car—a perky blue station wagon—out of the garage, and then Ben leant forward and opened the front passenger door for Elsie.

'I insist,' he said with a sweep of his arm when she started to back away. He blocked her path. Her choices were to plough through him or to subside into the front seat. She chose the latter.

'Hey, Meg.' He settled into the back seat.

'Hey, Ben.' She glanced at Elsie. 'Hello, Elsie.'

'Hello.'

He didn't need to see Elsie to know the precise way she'd just folded her hands in her lap.

'How was work?' he asked Meg as she turned the car in the direction of Nelson Bay. He was determined to hold up his end of the conversation this evening.

'Hectic…Fun.' She told them a silly story about one of the children there and then flicked a glance at Elsie. 'How was your day?'

'Fine.'

'What did you get up to?'

'Nothing new.'

In the rear vision mirror she caught Ben's glance and rolled her eyes.

'Though I did come across a recipe that I thought I might try. It's Indian. I've not tried Indian before.'

Silence—a stunned and at a loss silence—filled the car. Meg cleared her throat. 'Sounds…uh… great.' She glanced in the mirror again and Ben could almost see her mental shrug. She swallowed. 'What did *you* do today, Ben?'

'I bought some wood.'

She blinked as she stared at the road in front of her. 'Wood?'

'That's right. But don't ask me what it's for. It's a surprise.'

She glanced at Elsie. 'What's he up to? Is he building you a veggie patch?'

'Unlikely. But if he does it'll be *his* veggie patch.'

In the mirror Meg raised an eyebrow at him and he could read her mind. They were having a conversation like normal people—him, her and Elsie. He couldn't blame her for wondering if the sky was falling in.

'I'll tell you something that's surprised the pants off of me,' he said, as smoothly as he could.

In the mirror he watched her swallow. 'Don't keep me in suspense.'

'Elsie plays a mean hand of rummy.'

Meg glanced at her. 'You play rummy?'

'Yes, your father taught me.'

Just for a moment Meg's shoulders tightened, but then she rolled them and shrugged. 'Rummy is fun, but I prefer poker. Dad plays a mean hand of poker too.'

Did he? Ben wondered if he'd ever played a hand or two with his daughter.

'So Elsie kicked your butt, huh?'

'We're a game apiece. The tie-break's tonight.'

'Well, now.' Meg pulled the car to a halt in the RSL Club's parking lot. 'I expect to hear all about it tomorrow.'

'If she beats me, I'm making it the best of five.'

Elsie snorted. 'If you come to dinner next Wednesday, Meg, you can join in the fun.'

He wasn't sure who was more stunned by that offer—him, Meg or Elsie.

'Uh, right,' Meg managed. 'I'll look forward to it.'

Elsie's efforts at hospitality and conversation had thrown him as much as they'd obviously thrown Meg, but as Ben climbed out of the car he couldn't help wondering when he'd fallen into being so monosyllabic around his grandmother. Especially as he prided himself on being good company everywhere else.

He frowned and shook his head. He'd *never* been anything but monosyllabic around Elsie. It was a habit. One he hadn't even considered breaking until Meg had sent out the challenge.

He glanced at the older woman. When had she

got into the habit? Maybe nobody had ever challenged her, and—

Holy crap!

Ben's jaw dropped and his skin tightened when Meg rounded the car to join them. His chest expanded. It was as if he didn't fit his body properly any more.

Holy mackerel!

She wore a short blue skirt that stopped a good three inches above her knees and swished and danced about flirty thighs.

Man, Meg had great legs!

He managed to lift a hand to swipe it across his chin. No drool. He didn't do drool. Though, that said, until this week he'd have said he didn't do ogling Meg either.

Now it seemed he couldn't do anything else.

She had legs that went on for ever. The illusion was aided and abetted by the four-inch wedge heels she wore, the same caramel colour as her blouse. He toenails were painted a sparkly dark brown.

She nudged him in the ribs. 'What's with you?'

'I...um...' He coughed. Elsie raised an eyebrow and for the first time in his life he saw her actually smile. Oh, brilliant! She'd seen the lot and knew the effect Meg was having on him.

'I…um…' He cleared his throat and pointed to Meg's feet. 'Those shoes should come with a warning sign. Are you sure pregnant women are allowed to wear those things?'

She snorted. 'Just watch me, buster.'

He didn't have any other choice.

'I've given up caffeine, alcohol, salami and Camembert, but I'm not giving up my sexy sandals.'

She and Elsie set off for the club's entrance. He trailed after, mesmerised by the way Meg's hips swayed with hypnotic temptation.

How had he never noticed *that* before?

He swallowed. He had a feeling he was in for a long night.

CHAPTER SEVEN

MEG GLANCED AT Ben sitting at the table next to her in the club, and then away again before anyone could accuse her of having an unhealthy fixation with her best friend.

But tonight he'd amazed her. He not only made an effort to take part in the conversation, he actively promoted it. He quizzed her father on the key differences between five-card draw poker, stud poker and Texas hold 'em. She hadn't seen her father so animated in a long time. And Elsie listened in with a greedy avidity that made Meg blink.

The more she watched, the more she realised how good the older couple were for each other.

She bit her lip and glanced around the crowded dining room. She wanted to be happy for her father and Elsie. She gritted her teeth. She *was* happy for them. But their newfound vim made her chafe and burn. It made her hands clench.

Ben trailed a finger across one of her fists, leaving a burning path of awareness in his wake. She promptly unclenched it. He sent her a smile filled with so much understanding she wanted to lay her head on his shoulder and bawl her eyes out.

Pregnancy hormones.

Do you mean to use that as an excuse for every uncomfortable emotion that pummels you at the moment?

It might not explain her unexpected resentment towards the older couple, but it was absolutely positively the reason her pulse quickened and her skin prickled at the mere sight of Ben. It had to be. And it was absolutely positively the reason her stomach clenched when his scent slugged into her—that peculiar but evocative mixture of leather and Scotch whisky.

For pity's sake, he wasn't even wearing leather or drinking whisky.

Her lips twisted. He couldn't help it. He smelled like a bad boy—all illicit temptation and promises he wouldn't keep. That grin and his free and easy swagger promised heaven. For one night. She didn't doubt for a moment that he'd deliver on *that* particular promise either.

And darn it all if she didn't want a piece of that! She swallowed. She didn't just want it. She craved it. Her skin, her lungs, even her fingers ached with it.

Pregnancy hormones. *It had to be.*

Just her luck. Why couldn't she be like other women who became nauseous at the smell of frying bacon? That would be far preferable to feeling like *this* when Ben's scent hit her.

Her fingers curled into her palms. She had to find a way to resist all that seductive bad-boyness. For the sake of their friendship. And for the sake of her baby.

She dragged in a breath. She'd seen smart, sensible women make absolute fools of themselves over Ben and she had no intention of joining their ranks. She could *not* let lust deflect her from the important issue—ensuring her baby had the best possible life that she could give it. She could do that and save her friendship with Ben.

But not if she slept with him.

She ground her teeth together. Why had nobody warned her that being pregnant would make her... horny?

She shifted on her chair. Horny was the perfect description. There was nothing dignified and elegant or slow and easy in what she felt for Ben.

She risked a glance at him. Her blood Mexicanwaved in her veins. Heat pounded through her and she squeezed her thighs tightly together. What she felt for Ben—*her best friend*—was hot and carnal, primal and urgent.

And it had to be denied.

She dragged her gaze away and fiddled with her cutlery.

Ben nudged her and she could have groaned out loud as a fresh wave of leather and whisky slammed into her. But it occurred to her then that she'd left the entire running of the conversation up to him so far. He probably thought she was doing it to punish him, or to prove some stupid point, when the real reason was she simply couldn't string two thoughts let alone two sentences together in a coherent fashion.

'Sorry, I was a million miles away.' She made herself smile around the table. 'My girlfriends have warned me about baby brain.'

Ben cocked an eyebrow. He grinned that slow and easy grin that could reduce a woman to the consistency of warm honey, inch by delicious inch.

She swallowed and forced her spine to straighten. 'Basically it means my brain will turn to mush and I won't be able to verbalise anything but nonsense for days at a time.'

She glanced at Elsie. 'Do you remember that when you were pregnant?'

Elsie drew back, paled, and Meg tried not to wince. She'd never asked Elsie about pregnancy or motherhood before and it was obviously a touchy subject. She hadn't meant to be insensitive.

In an effort to remove attention from Elsie, she swung to her father. 'Or can *you* remember Mum having baby brain when she was pregnant with me?'

An ugly red flushed his cheeks. As if she'd reached across and slapped him across the face. Twice.

Oh, great. Another no-go zone, huh?

She wanted nothing more than to lay her head on the table, close her eyes and rest for a while.

'And what a sterling example of baby brain in action,' Ben murmured in her ear, and she found herself coughing back a laugh instead.

'I guess that's a no on both counts,' she managed, deciding to brazen it out, hoping it would make it less awkward all round. She glanced around the crowded dining room. 'There's a good crowd in but, man, I'm hungry. I wonder when our food will be ready?'

On cue, their table buzzer rang. Ben and her father shot to their feet. 'I'll get yours,' Ben told her, placing a hand on her shoulder to keep her in her seat.

Elsie watched as the two men walked towards the bistro counter where their plates waited. Meg made herself smile. 'Well, this is nice, isn't it?'

'You shouldn't have mentioned your mother.'

Meg blinked. 'Why ever not?'

Elsie pressed her lips primly together. 'He doesn't like to talk about her.'

Wasn't that the truth? 'And yet she was *my* mother and I do. Why should my needs be subordinate to his?'

'That's a selfish way to look at it.'

Interesting…Elsie was prepared to go into battle for her father. Something in Meg's heart lifted.

But something else didn't. 'Maybe I'm tired of stepping on eggshells and being self-sacrificing.'

Elsie paled. 'Meg, I—'

The men chose that moment to return with the food and Elsie broke off. Meg couldn't help but be relieved.

Ben glanced at Elsie and then whispered to Meg, 'More baby brain?'

'"Curiouser and curiouser," said Alice,' she returned.

He grinned. She grinned back. And for a moment everything was right again—she and Ben against the world…or at least against Elsie and Laurie, who'd been the world when she and Ben had been ten-year-olds.

They ate, and her father and Elsie reverted to their customary silence. Between them Meg and Ben managed to keep up a steady flow of chatter, but Meg couldn't help wondering if the older couple heard a word they said.

When they were finished, their plates removed and drinks replenished, Meg clapped her hands. 'Okay, I want to talk about the wedding for a moment.'

Her father scowled. 'I don't want a damn circus, Megan.'

'It's not going to be a circus. It's going to be a simple celebration. A celebration of the love you and Elsie share.' She folded her arms. 'And if you can't muster the courtesy to give each other that much respect then you shouldn't be getting married in the first place.'

Elsie and Laurie stared at her in shock. Ben let forth with a low whistle.

'Elsie—not this Saturday but the one after you and I are going shopping for your outfit.'

'Oh, but I don't need anything new.'

'Yes, you do. And so do I.' Her father had multiple suits, but... She turned to Ben. 'You'll need a suit.'

He saluted. 'I'm onto it.'

She turned back to the older couple. 'And you will both need an attendant. Who would you like as your bridesmaid and best man?'

Nobody said anything for a moment. She heaved back a sigh. 'Who were you going to have as your witnesses?'

'You and Ben,' her father muttered.

'Fine. I'll be your best man, but I'll be wearing a dress.'

'And I'll be bridesmaid in a suit,' Ben said to Elsie.

He said it without rancour and without wincing. He even said it with a grin on his face. Meg could have hugged him.

'Now, Elsie, do you want someone to give you away?'

'Of course not! Who on earth would I ask to do that?'

Meg leant back. She stared at the ceiling and counted to three. 'I'd have thought Ben would be the logical choice.'

The other woman's chin shot up. 'Ben? Do you really expect him to still be here in six weeks' time?'

'If he says he will, then, yes.'

'Give me away?' Her face darkened as she glared at Ben. 'Oh, you'd like that, wouldn't you? You'd love to give me away and be done with me for ever.'

Meg took one look at her best friend's ashen face and a scorching red-hot savagery shook through her. She leant forward, acid burning her throat and a rank taste filling her mouth. 'And who could blame him? I don't know why he even bothers with you at all. What the hell have you ever given him that he couldn't have got from strangers? You never show the slightest interest in his life, never show him the slightest affection—not even a tiny bit of warmth. You have no right to criticise him. *None!*'

'Meg.'

Ben's voice burned low but she couldn't stop. Even if she'd wanted to, she couldn't have. And she didn't want to. 'It was your job to show him love and security when he was just a little boy, but did you ever once hug him or tell him you were glad he'd come to stay with you? No, not once. Why not? He was a great kid and you…you're nothing but a—'

'Megan, that's enough! You will *not* speak to my intended like that.'

'Or what?' she shot straight back at her father. 'You'll never speak to me again? Well, seeing as you barely speak to me now, I can hardly see that'd be any great loss.'

Even as the words ripped out of her she couldn't believe she was uttering them. But she meant them. Every single one of them. And the red mist held her too much in its sway for her to regret them.

She might never regret them, but if she remained here she would say things she *would* regret—mean, bitter things just for the sake of it. She pushed out of her seat and walked away, walked right out of the club. She tramped the two blocks down to the water's edge to sit on a bench overlooking the bay as the sun sank in the west.

The walking had helped work off some of her anger. The warm air caressed the bare skin of her neck and legs, and the late evening light was as soothing as the ebb and flow of the water.

'Are you okay?'

Ben. And his voice was as soothing as the water

too. But it made her eyes prickle and sting. She nodded.

'Do you mind if I join you?'

She shook her head and gestured for him to take the seat beside her.

'What happened back there?' he finally asked. 'Baby brain?'

She didn't know if he was trying to make her laugh or if he was as honest-to-God puzzled as he sounded. She dragged in a breath that made her whole body shudder. 'That was honest, true-blue emotion, not baby brain. I've never told either one of them how I feel about our childhoods.'

'Well, you left them in no doubt about your feelings on the subject tonight.'

She glanced at him. 'I don't particularly feel bad about it.' Did that make her an awful person? 'I don't want revenge, and I don't want to ruin their happiness, but neither one of them has the right to criticise you or me for being unsupportive. Especially when we're bending over backwards for them.'

He rested his elbows on his knees and then glanced up at her. 'You've bottled that up for a long time. Why spill it now?'

She stared out at the water. The sky was quickly

darkening now that the sun had gone down. The burning started behind her eyes again. 'Now that I'm pregnant and expecting a child of my own, their emotional abandonment of us seems so much more unforgivable to me.'

He straightened and she turned to him.

'Ben, I can't imagine not making every effort for my child, regardless of what else is happening in my life. I love it so much already and it makes me see...'

'What?'

She had to swallow. 'It makes me see that neither one of them loved us enough.'

'Oh, sweetheart.' He slipped an arm about her shoulders and she leant against him, soaking up his strength and his familiarity, his *Ben*-ness.

'You've never blown your top like that,' she murmured into his chest. And he had so much more to breathe fire about than her—not just Elsie, but his mother and father too. 'Why not?' It obviously hadn't been healthy for *her* to bottle her anger and hurt up for so long. If he was bottling it up—

'Meg, honey.' He gave a low laugh. 'I did it with actions rather than words. Don't you remember?'

She thought about it for a while and then nodded. 'You rebelled big-time.' He'd started teenage binge-drinking at sixteen, and staying out until the wee small hours, getting into the occasional fight—and, she suspected, making himself at home in older women's beds.

The police had brought him home on more than one occasion. He'd had a couple of fathers and one husband warn him off—violently. Yes. She nodded again. Ben had gone off the rails in a big way, and she could see it now for the thumbing of his nose at his family that it had been.

Still, he'd had the strength and the sense to pull out of that downward spiral. Dave Clements—a local tour operator—had offered him a part-time job and had taken him under his wing, had encouraged Ben to finish school. And Ben had, and now he led the kind of life most people could only dream of.

But was he happy?

She'd thought so, but… She glanced up into his face and recognised the shadows there. She straightened and slipped her hand into his, held it tight. 'I'm sorry if my outburst brought up bad stuff for you. I didn't mean—'

'For me?' He swung to her. 'Hell, Meg, you were magnificent! I just…'

She swallowed. 'What?'

He released her to rest his elbows on his knees again and drag both hands back through his hair. She wanted his arm resting back across her shoulders. She wanted not to have hurt him.

'Is it my coming home and turning your nicely ordered plans on their head? Did that have a bearing on your outburst tonight? I don't mean to be causing you stress.'

'No! That had nothing to do with it. That—' she waved back behind her '—was about me and them. Not about me and you.' She moistened her lips. 'It was about me and my father.' And about her anger at Elsie for not having shown Ben any love or affection. 'You had nothing to do with that except in…'

'What?'

'When I was busy doing what you were mostly doing tonight,' she started slowly, 'making sure the conversation flowed and that there weren't any awkward moments, I didn't have the time to feel those old hurts and resentments.'

'While I, at least whenever I've been home,' he said with a delicious twist of his lips, 'have been far too busy stewing on them.'

'But when you took on my role tonight I started

to wonder why I was always so careful around them, and I realised what a lie it all seemed.'

'So you exploded.'

She slouched back against the bench. 'Why can't I just make it all go away and not matter any more? It all seems so pointless and self-defeating.' She couldn't change the past any more than she could change her father or Elsie. Her hands clenched. 'I should be able to just get over it.' She wasn't ten years old any more.

'It doesn't work like that.'

She knew he was right. She lifted her chin. 'It doesn't mean I have to let it blight the future, though. I don't have to continue mollycoddling my father or Elsie. At least not at the expense of myself.'

'No, you don't.'

He'd been telling her that for years. She'd never really seen what he meant till now.

'And I have a baby on the way.' She hugged herself. 'And that's incredibly exciting and it makes me happier than I have words for.'

He stared at her. He didn't smile. *They* had a baby on the way. *They*. She could read that in his face, but he didn't correct her.

She stared back out at the bay. The last scrap of

light in the sky had faded and house lights and boat
lights and street lights danced on the undulating
water, turning it into a kind of fairyland.

Only this wasn't a fairytale. Ben said he wanted
to be involved in their baby's life, but so far he
hadn't shown any joy or excitement—only agita-
tion and unease.

'So...?'

His word hung in the air. She didn't know what
it referred to. She hauled in a breath and raised one
shoulder. 'I don't much feel like going back to the
club and dealing with my father and Elsie.'

'You don't have to. I asked your father if he'd
see Elsie home.'

She swung back to him. 'I could kiss you!'

He grinned. A grin full of a slow burn that
melted her insides and sent need hurtling through
her. She started to reach for him, realised what she
was doing, and turned the questing touch into a
slap to his thigh before leaping to her feet.

'Feel like going for a walk?' She couldn't keep
sitting here next to him and not give in to temptation.

Which was crazy.

Truly crazy.

Nonetheless, walking was a much safer option.

With a shrug he rose and they set off along the boardwalk in the direction of the Nelson Bay marina, where there was a lot of distraction—lights and people and noise. Meg swallowed. Down at this end of the beach it was dark and almost deserted. It would take ten minutes to reach the marina. And then they'd have to walk back this way. In the dark and the quiet.

Her feet slowed.

But by then—after all that distraction and the exercise of walking—she'd have found a way to get her stupid hormones back under control, right?

She went to speed up again, but Ben took her arm and led her across a strip of grass and down to the sand. He kicked off his shoes, and after a moment's hesitation she eased her feet out of her wedges.

They paddled without talking very much. The water was warm. She needed icy cold rather than this beguiling warmth that brought all her senses dancing to life. Paddling with Ben in all the warmth of a late summer evening, with the scent of a nearby frangipani drenching the air, was far too intimate. Even though they'd done this a thousand times and it had never felt intimate before.

Except that one time after her high school graduation, when he'd been her white knight and taken her to the prom.

Don't think about that!

She cleared her throat. 'Tell me again how magnificent I was.' Maybe teasing and banter would help her find her way back to a more comfortable place.

Ben turned and moved back towards her. He inadvertently flicked up a few drops of water that hit her mid-calf...and higher. They beaded and rolled down her legs with delicious promise.

He halted in front of her, reaching out and cupping her cheek. 'Meg, nobody has ever stood up for me the way you did tonight. Not ever.'

In the moonlight his eyes shimmered. 'Oh, Ben,' she whispered, reaching up to cover his hand with hers. He deserved to have so many more people in his life willing to go out on a limb for him.

'You made me feel as if I could fly.'

She smiled. 'You mean you can't?'

He laughed softly and pulled her in close for a hug. She clenched her eyes shut and gritted her teeth as she forced her arms around him to squeeze him back for a moment. She started to release him, but he didn't release her. She rested her cheek on his shoulder and bit her lip until she tasted blood. It took all her concentration to keep her hands where they ought to be.

And then his hand slid down her back and it wasn't a between-friends gesture. It was...

She drew back to glance into his face. The hunger and the need reflected in his eyes made her sway towards him. She planted her hands against his chest to keep her balance, to keep from falling against him. As soon as she regained her footing she meant to push him away.

Only, her hands, it seemed, had a different idea altogether. They slid across his shirt, completely ignoring the pleasant sensation of soft cotton to revel in the honed male flesh beneath it. Ben's chest had so much *definition*. And he was hot! His heat branded her through his shirt and his heart beat against her palm like a dark throbbing promise. The pulse in her throat quivered.

She swallowed and tried to catch her breath. She should move away.

But the longer she remained in the circle of Ben's arms, the more the strength and the will drained from her body and the harder it became to think clearly and logically.

And beneath her hands his body continued to beat at her like a wild thing—a tempting and tempestuous primal force, urging her to connect with something wild and elemental within herself.

She lifted her gaze to his. A light blazed from his eyes, revealing his need, an unchecked recklessness and his exaltation.

'I've been fighting this all night,' he rasped, 'but I'm not going to fight it any more.'

He tangled his hand in her hair and pulled it back until her lips lifted, angled just so to give him maximum access, and then his mouth came down on hers—hot, hungry, unchecked.

His lips laid waste to all her preconceptions. She'd thought he'd taste wickedly illicit and forbidden, but he didn't taste like whisky or leather or midnight. He tasted like summer and ripe strawberries and the tang of the ocean breeze. He tasted like freedom.

It was more intoxicating than anything she'd ever experienced.

Kissing Ben was like flying.

A swooping, swirling, tumbling-in-the-surf kind of flying.

He pulled her closer, positioned his body in such a way that it pressed against all the parts of her she most wanted touched—but it didn't appease her, only inflamed. His name ripped from her throat and he took advantage of it to deepen the kiss further. She followed his lead, drinking him in greedily. Her head swam. She fisted her hands in his shirt and dragged him closer. His strength was the only thing keeping them both upright.

She needed him *now*. Her body screamed for him. She pressed herself against him in the most shameless way she could—pelvis to pelvis, making it clear what she wanted. Demanding fulfilment.

His mouth lifted from hers. He dragged in air and then his teeth grazed her throat. She arched against him. 'Please, Ben. Please.' she sobbed.

With a growl, he scrunched her skirt in his hand. He traced the line of her panty elastic with one finger and she thought she might explode then and there.

His finger shifted, slid beneath the elastic.

Oh, please. Please.

A car horn blared, renting the air with discord, and Ben leapt away from her so fast she'd have fallen if he hadn't shot out an arm to steady her. When she regained her balance he released her with an oath that burned her ears.

'What the *hell* were you thinking?' His finger shook as he pointed it at her.

Same as you. Only she couldn't get her tongue to work properly and utter that remark out loud.

He wheeled away, dragging both hands back through his hair.

No, no, no, she wanted to wail. *Don't turn knight on me now—you're a bad boy!*

But when he swung back his face was tense and drawn, and she was grateful she hadn't said it out loud.

Because it would have been stupid.

And wrong.

Her flesh chilled. Trembling set in. She walked away from him and up the beach a little way to sit. She needed to think. And she couldn't think and walk at the same time because her limbs were boneless and it took all her concentration to remain upright. She pulled her skirt down as far as it would go and kept her legs flat out in front of her to reveal as little thigh as possible.

He strode up to her and punched a finger at her again. 'This is not on, Meg. You and me. It's never going to happen.'

'Don't use that tone with me.' She glared at him. 'You started it.'

'You could've said no!'

'You could've not kissed me in the first place!'

She expected him to stride away into the night, but he didn't. He paced for a bit and then eventually came back and sat beside her. But not too close.

'Are we still okay?' he growled.

'Sure we are.' But her throat was tight.

'I don't know what came over me.'

'It's been an emotional evening.' She swallowed. 'And when emotions run high you always seek a physical outlet.'

He nodded. There was a pause. 'It's not usually your style, though.'

She shifted, rolled her shoulders. 'Yeah, well, it seems that being pregnant has made me…itchy.'

He stared. And then he leaned slightly away from her. 'You're joking?'

'I wish I were.'

She had to stop looking at him. She forced her gaze back to the front—to the gently lapping water of the bay. Which wasn't precisely the mood she was after. She forced her gaze upwards. Stars. She heaved out a sigh and gave up.

'So you're feeling…? Umm…? All of the time?'

She pressed her hands to her cheeks and stared doggedly out at the water, desperately wishing for some of its calm to enter her soul. 'I expected to feel all maternal and Mother Earthy. Not sexy.'

'You know, it kind of makes sense,' he said after a bit. 'All those pregnancy hormones are making you look great.'

At the moment she'd take the haggard morning sickness look if it would get things between her and Ben on an even keel again.

'You sure we're okay?' he said again.

She bit back a sigh. 'I'm not going to fall for you, Ben, if that's what you're worried about.'

'No, I—'

'For a start, I don't like the way you treat women, and I'm sure as hell not going to let any man treat me like that.'

'I do not treat women badly,' he growled.

'Wham, bam, thank you, ma'am. That's your style.'

And as far as she was concerned it was appalling. She grimaced. Even if a short time ago she'd been begging for exactly that. She massaged her temples. She found her own behaviour this evening appalling too. She'd never acted like that before—so heedless and mindless. Not with any man.

'I haven't had any complaints.'

She snorted. 'Because you don't stick around long enough to hear them.'

'Hell, Meg.' He scowled. 'I show a woman a good time. I don't make promises.'

But he didn't care if a woman did read more into their encounter. He'd used that to his advantage on more than one occasion.

'Yeah, well, I want more than that from a relationship, and that's something I know you're not in the market for.' He grabbed her arm when she went to rise. She fell back to the sand, her shoulder jostling his. 'What?'

He let her go again. 'I'm glad we're on the same page, because...'

An ache started up behind her eyes. 'Because?'

'I've made a decision and we need to talk about it.'

She smoothed her skirt down towards her knees again. Ben was going to leave right after the wedding. That was what he wanted to tell her, wasn't it?

She pulled in a breath and readied herself for his news. It was good news, she told herself, straightening her spine and setting her shoulders. Things could get back to normal again.

'I've made the decision to stay in Port Stephens. I'll find work here and I'll find a place to live. I want to be a father to our baby, Meg. A *proper* father.'

CHAPTER EIGHT

THE WORLD TILTED to one side. Meg planted a hand against shifting sand. 'Staying?' Her voice wobbled.

Living here in Port Stephens, so close to Elsie and his childhood, would make Ben miserable. She closed her eyes. In less than six months he'd go stir crazy and flee in a trail of dust.

And where would that leave her baby and their friendship?

Depending on how much under the six-month mark Ben managed to hold on for, her baby might not even have been born. She opened her eyes. In which case it wouldn't have come to rely on Ben or to love him.

It wouldn't be hurt by his desertion.

But Ben would be. His failure to do this would destroy something essential in him.

And she didn't want to bear witness to that.

She turned to find him studying her. His shoulders were hitched in a way that told her he was waiting for her to say something hard and cruel.

And the memory of their kiss—that bone-crushing kiss—throbbed in all the spaces between them.

She moistened her lips. 'You haven't been back here a full week yet. This is a big decision—huge. It's life-changing. You don't have to rush it, or make a hasty choice, or—'

'When it comes down to brass tacks, Meg, the decision itself is remarkably simple.'

It was?

'Being a parent—a father—is the most important job in the world.'

Her heart pounded. He would hate himself—*hate*—when he found out he wasn't up to the task. Her heart burned, her eyes ached and her temples throbbed.

And at the back of her mind all she could think about was kissing him again. Kissing him had been a mistake. But that didn't stop her from wanting to repeat it.

And repeat it.

Over and over again.

But if they did it would destroy their friendship. She clenched her hands in her lap and battled the need to reach out and touch him again, kiss him again, as she hungered to do.

'Coming back home this time…' He glanced down at his hands. 'I've started to realise how shallow my life really is.'

Her jaw dropped.

'I know it looks exciting, and I guess it is. But it's shallow too. I've spent my whole life running away from responsibility. I'm starting to see I haven't achieved anything of real value at all.'

She straightened. 'That's not true. You help people achieve their dreams. You give them once-in-a-lifetime experiences—stories they can tell their children.'

'And who am I going to tell *my* stories to?'

Her heart started to thud.

'I've steered clear of any thoughts of children in my future, afraid I'd turn out like my parents.' His face grew grim but his chin lifted. 'That will only happen if I let it.'

He turned to her. *Stop thinking about kissing him!*

'What I really want to know is what you're scared of, Meg. Why does the thought of my coming home for good and being a father to our child freak you out?'

Because what if I never do manage to get my hormones back under control?

She snapped away at that thought. It was ludicrous. And unworthy. This should have nothing to do with her feelings and everything to do with her baby's. She couldn't let how she felt colour that reality.

'Meg?'

The notion of Ben coming home for good *did* freak her out. It scared her to the soles of her feet. He knew her too well for her to deny it. 'I don't want to hurt you,' she whispered.

He set his shoulders in a rigid line. 'Give it to me straight.'

She glanced at her hands. She hauled in a breath. 'I'm afraid you'll hang around just long enough for the baby to love you. I'm afraid the baby will come to love and rely on you but you won't be able to hack the monotony of domesticity. I'm afraid your restlessness will get the better of you and you'll leave. And if you do that, Ben, you will break my baby's heart.'

He flinched. The throbbing behind her eyes intensified.

'And if you do that, Ben…' she forced herself to continue '…I don't know if I could ever forgive you.'

And they would both lose the most important friendship of their lives.

He shot to his feet and strode down to the water's edge.

'And what's more,' she called after him, doing what she could to keep her voice strong, 'if that's the way this all plays out, I think you will hate yourself.'

There was so much to lose if he stayed.

He strode back to where she sat, planted his feet in front of her. 'I can't do anything about your fears, Meg. I'm sorry you feel the way you do. I know I have no one to blame but myself, and that only time will put your fears to rest.' He dragged a hand back through his hair. 'But when *our* baby is born I'm going to be there for it every step of the way. I want it to love me. I want it to rely on me. I'll be doing everything to make that happen.'

She shrank from him. 'But—'

'I mean to be the best father I can be. I mean to be the kind of father to my son or daughter that my father wasn't to me. I want our baby to have everything good in life, and I mean to stick around to make sure that happens.'

Meg covered her face with her hands. 'Oh, Ben, I'm sorry. I'm so, so sorry.'

* * *

Ben stared at Meg, with her head bowed and her shoulders slumped, and knelt down on the sand beside her, his heart burning. He pulled her hands from her face. 'What on earth are you sorry for?' She didn't have anything to be sorry about.

'I'm sorry I asked you to donate sperm. I'm sorry I've created such an upheaval in your life. I didn't mean for that to happen. I didn't mean to turn your life upside down.'

The darkness in her eyes, the guilt and sorrow swirling in their depths, speared into him. 'I know that.' He sat beside her again. 'When I agreed to be your sperm donor I had no idea I'd feel this way, and I'm sorry that's turned all your plans on their head.'

She pulled in a breath that made her whole body shudder. He wanted to wrap her in his arms. She moved away as if she'd read that thought in his face. It was only an inch, but it was enough. *All because of that stupid kiss.*

Why the hell had he kissed her? He clenched a hand. Ten years ago he'd promised he would never do that again. Ten years ago, when that jerk she'd been dating had dumped her. She'd been vulnerable then. She'd been vulnerable tonight too. And he'd taken advantage of that fact.

Meg wasn't the kind of girl a guy kissed and then walked away from. He might be staying in Port Stephens for good, but he wasn't changing his life *that* much. He had to stop sending her such mixed signals. They were friends. *Just* friends. *Best friends.*

He closed his eyes and gritted his teeth. Control—he needed to find control.

And he needed to forget how divine she'd felt in his arms and how that kiss had made him feel like a superhero, shooting off into the sky.

She cleared her throat, snagging his attention again. 'Obviously neither one of us foresaw what would happen.'

Her sigh cut him to the quick. 'I know this is hard for you, Meg, but I do mean to be a true father to our child.'

She still didn't believe him. It was in her face. In the way she opened her hands and let the sand trickle out of them. In the way she turned to stare out at the water.

'And because I do want to be a better father than my own, I need to clear the air about that kiss.'

His body heated up in an instant as the impact

of their kiss surged through him again. That kiss had been—

He fisted his hands and tried to cut the memory from his mind. He was not going to dwell on that kiss again. *Ever.* He couldn't. Not if he wanted to maintain his sanity. Not if he wanted to save their friendship.

Meg slapped her hands to the sides of her knees. 'You are nothing like your father.'

How could she be so sure of that?

'You would never, *ever* put a gun to anyone's head—let alone your own child's.'

Bile rose in his throat. That had happened nearly twenty years ago, but the day and all its horror was etched on his memory as if with indelible ink. His mother and father had undergone one of the most acrimonious divorces in the history of man. In the custody battle that had ensued they had used their only son to score as many points off one another as they could. At every available opportunity.

Their bitterness and their hate had turned them into people Ben hadn't been able to recognise. They'd pushed and pushed and pushed each other, until one day his father had shown up on the front doorstep with a shotgun.

Ben's heart pounded. He could still taste the fear

in his mouth when he'd first caught sight of the gun—could still feel the grip of a hard hand on the back of his neck when he'd turned to run. He'd been convinced his father would kill them.

Ben pressed a hand to his forehead and drew oxygen into his lungs. Meg wrapped her arm through his. It helped anchor him back in the present moment, drawing him out of that awful one twenty years ago.

'My parents must've cared for each other once— maybe even loved each other—but marriage for them resulted in my father being in prison and my mother dumping me with Elsie and never being heard from again.'

'Not all marriages end like that, Ben.'

'True.'

But he had the same raging passions inside him that his parents had. He had no intention of setting them free. That was why he kept his interludes with women light and brief. It was safer all round.

Gently, he detached his arm from Meg's. 'Whatever else I do, though, marriage is something I'm never going to risk.'

She shook her head and went back to lifting sand and letting it trickle through her hand. 'This is one of those circular arguments that just go round and round without ending. We agreed to disagree about this years ago.'

He heard her unspoken question. *So why bring it up now?*

'Regardless of what you think, Meg, I do mean to be a good father. But that doesn't mean I've changed my mind about marriage.'

She stopped playing with the sand. 'And you think because I'm feeling a little sexy that I'm going to weave you into my fantasies and cast you in the role of handsome prince?' She snorted. 'Court jester, more like. It'd take more than a kiss for me to fall in love with you, Ben Sullivan. I may have baby brain, but that doesn't mean I've turned into a moron. Especially—' she shot to her feet '—when I don't believe you'll hang around long enough for anyone to fall in love with you anyway.'

He didn't argue the point any further. Only time would prove to her that he really did mean to stick around.

He scrambled to his feet. He just had to make sure he didn't kiss her again. Meg didn't do one-night stands—it wasn't how she was built inside. She got emotionally involved. He knew that. He'd always known that. He pushed his shoulders back and shoved his hands into the pockets of his shorts.

He'd made a lot of mistakes in his sorry life, but he wasn't making that one.

He set off after Meg. 'What would you like me to do in relation to the wedding this week?'

She'd walked back to where they'd kicked off their shoes. He held her arm as she slid hers back on. He gritted his teeth in an effort to counter the warm temptation of her skin.

She blinked up at him as she slid a finger around the back of one of her sandals. She righted herself and moved out of his grasp. 'There's still a lot to do.' She glanced at him again. 'How busy are you this coming week?'

He'd be hard at work, casting around for employment opportunities, putting out feelers and sifting through a few preliminary ideas he'd had, but he'd find time to help her out with this blasted wedding. The days of leaving everything up to her were through. 'I have loads of time.'

'Well, for a start, I need those names from Elsie.'

'Right.'

They set off back towards the club and Meg's car. 'I don't suppose you'd organise the invitations, would you? I wasn't going to worry with anything too fancy. I was just going to grab a few packets of nice invitations from the newsagents and write

them out myself. Calligraphy is unnecessary—
they just need to be legible.'

'Leave it to me.'

'Thank you. That'll be a big help.'

'Anything else?'

'I would be very, very grateful if you could find
me a gardener. I just don't have the spare time to
keep on top of it at the moment. This wedding will
be that garden's last hurrah, because I'm having
all those high-maintenance annuals ripped out and
replaced with easy-care natives.'

He nodded. 'Not a problem.'

They drove home in silence. When Meg turned
in at her driveway and turned off the ignition she
didn't invite him in for a drink and he didn't suggest it either. Instead, with a quick goodnight, he
headed next door.

The first thing he saw when he entered the
kitchen was Elsie, sitting at the table shuffling a
deck of cards. Without a word, she dealt out a hand
for rummy. Ben hesitated and then sat.

'How's Meg?'

'She's fine.'

'Good.'

He shifted. 'She'd feel a whole lot happier,

though, if you'd give her a list of ten people she can invite to the wedding.'

Elsie snorted. He blinked again. Had that been a *laugh*?

'She said that although her father won't admit it, he'd like more than a registry office wedding.'

Elsie snorted again, and this time there was no mistaking it—it was definitely a laugh. 'I'll make a deal with you, Ben.'

Good Lord. The woman was practically garrulous. 'A deal?'

'For every hand you win, I'll give you a name.'

He straightened on his chair. 'You're on.'

Meg glanced around at a tap on the back door. And then froze. Ben stood there, looking devastatingly delicious, and a traitorous tremor weakened her knees.

With a gulp, she waved him in. Other than a couple of rushed conversations about the wedding, she hadn't seen much of him during the last two weeks. Work had been crazy, with two of her staff down with the flu, and whenever she had seen Ben and asked what he'd been up to he'd simply answered with a cryptic, 'I've been busy.' Long, leisurely conversations obviously hadn't been on either of their agendas.

Her gaze lowered to his lips. Lips that had caressed hers. Lips that had transported her to a place beyond herself and made her yearn for more. So much more. Lips that were moving now.

'Whatever it is you're cooking, Meg, no known man would be able to resist it.'

She snapped away and forced a smile.

'Cookies?'

Her smile became almost genuine at the hope in his voice. 'Chocolate chip,' she confirmed.

'Even better.' He glanced at her baking companions. 'Sounds like you guys have been having fun in here.'

Loss suddenly opened up inside her. He was her best friend. They had to find a way to overcome this horrid awkwardness.

She swallowed and hauled in a breath, gestured to the two children. 'This is Laura, who is ten, and Lochie, who is eight.'

'We're brother and sister,' Laura announced importantly.

'And Auntie Meg used to go to school with Mummy.'

'Felicity Strickland,' Meg said at his raised

eyebrow. 'Laura and Lochie—this is my friend Ben from next door. He went to school with your mummy too. What do you think? Will we let him share our cookies?'

Lochie nodded immediately. 'That means there'll be another boy.'

In Lochie's mind another boy meant an ally, and Meg had a feeling he was heartily sick of being bossed by his sister.

Laura folded her arms. 'He'll have to work for them. It's only fair, because we've all worked.'

Meg choked back a laugh. She half expected Ben to make some excuse and back out through the door.

'What would I have to do?' he asked Laura instead. 'I'll do just about anything for choc-chip cookies. Especially ones that smell this good.'

Laura glanced up at Meg.

'How about Ben sets the table?'

'And pours the milk?'

She nodded. 'Sounds fair.'

Ben tackled setting the table and pouring out four glasses of milk while Meg pulled a second tray of cookies from the oven and set them to cool on the counter. She'd hoped that baking cookies would make her feel super-maternal, but one glance at Ben threw that theory out of the water.

She still felt—

Don't think about it!

Her hands shook as she placed the first batch of cookies on a plate and handed them to Laura, who took them over to the table.

They ate cookies and drank milk.

But even over the home-baked goodness of choc-chip cookies Meg caught a hint of leather and whisky. She tried to block it from her mind, tried to ignore the longing that burned through her veins.

The children regaled Ben with stories of their Christmas trip to Bali. Meg glanced at Ben and then glanced away again, biting her lip. It was no use telling herself this was just Ben. There was no *just* Ben about it—only a hard, persistent throb in her blood and an ache in her body.

When the phone rang she leapt to her feet, eager for distraction.

Ben's eyes zeroed in on her face the moment she returned to the kitchen. 'Problem?'

She clenched and unclenched her hands. 'The caterers I had lined up for the wedding have cancelled on me, the rotten—' she glanced at the children '—so-and-sos.'

She pressed her fingers to her temples and paced up and down on the other side of the breakfast bar. The wedding was three weeks away. Less than that. Two weeks and six days. Not that she was counting or anything.

Ben stood. 'What can I do?'

She glanced at him. She glanced at the children. A plan—devious, and perhaps a little unfair—slid beneath her guard. No, she couldn't.

Two weeks and six days.

She folded her arms. 'Are you up for a challenge, Ben Sullivan?'

He rocked back on his heels. 'What kind of challenge?'

She glanced at the children and then back at him, with enough meaning in her face that he couldn't possibly mistake her message.

He folded his arms too. 'Bring it on.'

'If you keep Laura and Lochie amused for an hour or two, it'll give me a chance to ring around and find a replacement caterer.'

He glanced at the television. 'Not a problem.'

She shook her head and glanced out of the kitchen window towards the back yard. There was no mistaking the panic that momentarily filled his eyes. 'I'll need peace and quiet.'

Did he even know the first thing about children and how much work they could sometimes be? Laura truly was the kind of child designed to test Ben's patience to the limit too. And when he found out the truth that being a father wasn't all beer and skittles—all fun and laughter at the beach and I-love-you-Daddy cuddles—how long before he left?

She did what she could to harden her heart, to stop it from sinking, to cut off its protests.

Lochie's face lit up. 'Can we go to the beach? Can we go swimming?'

Relief lit Ben's face too, but Meg shook her head. 'Your mum said no swimming.' Besides, she wanted them all here, right under her nose, where she could keep an eye on them.

Ben glared at her. 'Why not?'

She reached out and brushed a hand through Lochie's hair, pulled him against her in a hug. 'Lochie's recovering from an ear infection.'

Ben shuffled his feet. 'I'm sorry to hear that, mate.'

Lochie straightened. 'We could play Uno. Laura remembered to bring it.'

'Because you *didn't*.' She rolled her eyes. 'You

never do. Do you know how to play?' she demanded of Ben.

'No idea.'

'Then I'll teach you.' She took Ben's hand. 'Get the game, Lochie.'

'Please,' Ben corrected.

Laura blinked. So did Meg. 'Get the game, *please*, Lochie,' Laura amended, leading both males outside as she waxed lyrical about the importance of good manners.

Meg grimaced. Poor Ben. Laura was ten going on eighty. It hardly seemed fair to expect him to cope with her. She glanced down at her baby bump, rested her hand on it before glancing back out of the window. It was an hour. Two hours tops. She'd be nearby, and if he couldn't deal with Laura for that length of time then he had no right remaining here in Port Stephens at all.

Still, even with that decided Meg couldn't move from the window. She watched as the trio settled on the outdoor furniture, and as Ben listened while Laura explained the rules of the game in exhaustive detail. His patience touched her. Once the game started he kept both children giggling so hard she found herself wishing she could go outside and join them.

She shook her head. Two weeks and six days. She had a caterer to find.

It took Meg forty minutes' worth of phone calls before she found a replacement caterer. She glanced at her watch and winced. How on earth was Ben surviving? She raced into the family room to peer out through the glass sliding door that afforded an excellent view of the back yard and started to laugh.

Ben had set up an old slip 'n' slide of hers—one they'd played on when they were children—and the three of them were having the time of their lives. Laura giggled, Lochie chortled, and Ben's whole face had come alive. It shone.

She took a step towards the door, transfixed, her hand reaching out to rest against the glass as if reaching for...

Ben's face shone.

Her other hand moved to cover her stomach. What if Ben *did* stay? What if he kept his word and found fatherhood satisfying? What if he didn't run away?

Her heart thudded as she allowed the idea truly to sink in. The blood vessels in her hand pulsed against the glass. If Ben kept his word then her baby would have a father.

A real father.

She snatched her hand away. She backed up to the sofa. But she couldn't drag her gaze away from the happy trio in her back yard, watching in amazement as Ben effortlessly stepped in to prevent a spat between the children. He had them laughing again in no time. The man was a natural.

And he had a butt that—

She waved a hand in front of her face to shoo the thought away. She didn't have time for butts—not even butts as sublime as Ben's.

Or chests. She blinked and leaned forward. He really did have the most amazing body. He'd kept his shirt on, but it was now so wet it stuck to him like a second skin, outlining every delicious muscle and—

She promptly changed seats and placed her back to the door. She dragged in a breath and tried to control the crazy beating of her heart.

If Ben *did* overcome his wanderlust...

She swallowed. He'd never lied to her before. Why would he lie to her now? Especially about something as important as their child's happiness.

No! She shot to her feet. *Her* child!

She raced to the refrigerator to pour herself an ice-cold glass of water, but when she tipped her head back to drink it her eyes caught on the vivid blue of the water slide and the children's laughter filled her ears.

Slowly she righted her glass. This was their child. *Theirs.* She'd let fear cloud her judgement. Not fear for the baby, but fear for herself. Fear that this child might somehow damage her friendship with Ben. Fear that she might come to rely on him too heavily. Fear at having to share her child.

She abandoned her water to grip her hands together. She hadn't expected to share this baby. In her possessiveness, was she sabotaging Ben's efforts?

She moistened suddenly dry lips. It would be hard, relinquishing complete control and having to consider someone else's opinions and ideas about the baby, but behind that there would be a sense of relief too, and comfort. To know she wasn't in this on her own, that someone else would have her and the baby's backs.

She'd fully expected to be a single mum—had been prepared for it. But if she didn't have to go it alone...

If her baby could have a father...

Barely aware of what she was doing, Meg walked back to the double glass doors. Ben had a child under each arm and he was swinging them round and round until they shrieked with laughter. Laura broke away to grab the hose and aimed it directly at his chest. He clutched at the spot as if shot and fell down, feigning injury. Both children immediately pounced on him.

The longer Meg watched them the clearer the picture in her mind became. Her baby could have a mother *and* a father. Her baby could have it all!

Pictures formed in her mind—pictures of family picnics and trips to the beach, of happy rollicking Christmases, of shared meals and quiet times when the baby was put down and—

She snapped away. Heat rushed through her. *Get a grip!* Her baby might have a father, but that didn't mean she and Ben would form a cosy romantic bond and become the ideal picture-perfect family. That would never happen.

Her heart pounded so hard it almost hurt, and she had to close her eyes briefly until she could draw much needed breath into straining lungs.

Ben would never do family in the way she wanted or needed. That stupid kiss ten years ago and the way Ben had bolted from town afterwards had only reinforced what she'd always known—that he would never surrender to the unpredictability and raw emotion of romantic love, with all its attendant highs and lows. She might have baby brain and crazy hormones at the moment, but she'd better not forget that fact—not for a single, solitary moment.

Best friends.

She opened her eyes and nodded. They were best friends who happened to have a child together and they'd remain friends. They *could* make this work.

She rested her forehead against the glass, her breath fogging it so she saw the trio dimly, through a haze. If only she knew for certain that Ben wouldn't leave, that he wouldn't let them down. That he'd stay. She wanted a guarantee, but there weren't—

She froze.

She turned to press her back against the door. What did Ben want more than anything else in the world?

To be on the crew of a yacht that was sailing around the world.

Did he want that more than he wanted to be a father?

Her heart pounded. Her stomach churned. She pushed away from the door and made for the

phone, dialling the number for Dave Clements'
travel agency. 'Dave? Hi, it's Meg.'

'Hey, Meg. Winnie and I are really looking forward to the wedding. How are the preparations
coming along?'

'Oh, God, don't ask.'

He laughed. 'If there's anything I can do?'

'Actually, I do need to come in and talk to you
about organising a honeymoon trip for the happy
couple.'

'Drop in any time and we'll put together something fabulous for them.'

'Thank you.' She swallowed. 'But that's not the
reason I called.' Her mouth went dry. She had to
swallow again. 'I've been racking my brain, trying to come up with a way to thank Ben. He's been
such a help with the preparations and everything.'

'And?'

'Look,' she started in a rush, 'you know he's always wanted to crew on a round-the-world yacht
expedition? I wondered if there was a way you
could help me make that happen?'

A whistle travelled down the line. She picked
up a pen and doodled furiously on the pad by the
phone, concentrating on everything but her desire
to retract her request.

'Are you sure that's what you want, Meg? When I spoke to him through the week it sounded like he was pretty set on staying in Port Stephens.'

She glanced out of the window at Ben and the children. Still laughing. Still having the time of their lives. 'It's something he's always wanted. I want him to at least have the opportunity to turn it down.'

But would he?

'Okay, leave it with me. I'll see what I can do.'

'Thanks, Dave.'

She replaced the receiver. If Ben turned the opportunity down she'd have her guarantee.

If he didn't?

She swallowed. Well, at least that would be an answer too.

CHAPTER NINE

BEN CRUISED THE road between Nelson Bay and Fingal Bay with the driver's window down, letting the breeze dance through the car and ruffle his hair. He put his foot down a centimetre and then grinned in satisfaction. This baby, unlike his motorbike, barely responded.

Perfect.

The coastal forest and salt-hardy scrubland retreated as the road curved into the small township. On impulse he parked the car and considered the view.

As a kid, he'd loved the beach. He and Meg had spent more time down there than they had in their own homes. Maybe he'd taken it for granted. Or maybe he'd needed to leave it for a time to see some of the world's other beautiful places before he could come back and truly appreciate it.

Because Meg was right—for sheer beauty, Fingal Bay was hard to beat. The line of the beach, the rocky outcrop of Fingal Island directly opposite and the sand spit leading out to it formed a cradle that enclosed the bay on three of its sides. The unbelievably clear water revealed the sandy bottom of the bay, and the bottle-nosed dolphins that were almost daily visitors.

He'd fled this place as soon as he was of a legal age. Staring at it now, he felt as if it welcomed him back. He dragged in a breath of late-afternoon air—salt-scented and warm—then glanced at his watch and grinned. Meg should be home by now.

He drove to her house, pulled the car into her driveway and blared the horn. He counted to five before her front door swung open.

Meg stood silhouetted in the light with the darkness of the house behind her and every skin cell he possessed tightened. Her baby bump had grown in the month he'd been home. He gazed at it hungrily. He gazed at *her* hungrily.

He gave himself a mental slap upside the head. He'd promised to stop thinking about Meg that way. He'd promised not to send her any more mixed messages. He would never be able to give her all the things a woman like her wanted and needed, and he valued their friendship too much to pretend otherwise.

If only it were as easy as it sounded.

With a twist of his lips, he vaulted out of the car.

When she saw him, her jaw dropped. She stumbled down the driveway to where he stood, her mouth opening and closing, her eyes widening. 'What on earth is that?'

He grinned and puffed out his chest. 'This—' he slapped the bonnet '—is my new car.' This would prove to her that he was a changed man, that he was capable of responsibility and stability. That he was capable of fatherhood.

He pushed his hands into the pockets of his jeans, his shoulders free and easy, while he waited for her to finish her survey of the car and then pat him on the back and meet his gaze with new respect in her eyes.

'You...' She swallowed. 'You've bought a station wagon?'

'I have.' His grin widened. He'd need room for kid stuff now. And this baby had plenty of room.

'You've gone and bought an ugly, boxy *white* station wagon?'

She stared at him as if he'd just broken out in green and purple spots. His shoulders froze in place. So did his grin. She planted her hands on her hips and glared. The sun picked out the golden highlights in her hair. Her eyes blazed, but her lips were the sweetest pink he'd ever seen.

Meg was hot. He shifted, adjusting his jeans. Not just pretty, but smokin' hot. Knock-a-man-off-his-feet hot. He needed something ice-cold to slake the heat rising through him or he'd—

'Where's your bike?' she demanded.

He moistened his lips. 'I traded it.' The icy sting of the cold current that visited the bay at this time of year might do the trick.

'You. Did. *What?*' Her voice rose on the last word. Her nostrils flared. She poked him in the shoulder. 'Have you gone mad? What on earth were you thinking?'

He leant towards her, all his easy self-satisfaction slaughtered. 'I was trying to prove to you that I've changed,' he ground out. 'This car is a symbol that I can be a good father.'

'It shows you've lost your mind!'

She dragged both hands back through her hair. She stared at him for a moment, before transferring her gaze back to the station wagon.

'Inside—now,' she ordered. 'I don't want to have this conversation on the street.'

He planted his feet. 'I'm not some child you can order about. If you want to talk to me, then you can ask me like a civilised person. I'm tired of you treating me like a second-class citizen.' Like someone who couldn't get one damn thing right.

He knew she was stressed about the wedding, about the baby, about him—about that damn kiss!—but he was through with taking this kind of abuse from her. Meg had always been a control freak, but she was getting worse and it was time she eased up.

He welcomed the shock in her eyes, but not the pain that followed swiftly on its heels. Meg was a part of him. Hurting her was like hurting himself.

She swallowed and nodded. 'Sorry, that really was very rude of me. It's just…I think we need to talk about that.' She gestured to his car. 'Would you come inside for coffee so we can discuss it?' When he didn't say anything she added, 'Please?'

He nodded and followed her into the house.

She glanced at the kitchen clock. 'Coffee or a beer?'

'Coffee, thanks.' Meg had been right about the drinking. Somewhere along the line, when he hadn't been paying attention, it had become a habit. He'd made an effort to cut back.

She made coffee for him and decaf for herself. He took in the tired lines around her eyes and mouth and the pallor of her skin where previously there'd been a golden glow and something snagged in his chest. 'What's wrong with the car?' he said, accepting the mug she handed him. 'I thought it would show you I'm serious about sticking around and being involved with the baby.'

'I think I've been unfair to you on that, Ben.'

She gestured to the family room sofas and he followed her in a daze.

She sat. She didn't tuck her legs beneath her like she normally did. She didn't lean back against the sofa's cushioned softness. She perched on the edge of the seat, looking weary and pale. Her mug sat on the coffee table, untouched. He wanted to ease her back into that seat and massage her shoulders...or her feet. Whichever would most help her to relax.

Except he had a no-touching-Meg rule. And he wasn't confident enough in his own strength to break it.

She glanced up, the green in her eyes subdued. 'You said you wanted to be an involved father and I automatically assumed...'

'That I was lying.'

'Not on purpose, no.' She frowned. 'But I didn't think you really knew what you were talking about.

I didn't think you understood the reality of what you were planning to do.'

And why should she? The truth was he hadn't understood the reality at all. Not at first.

She glanced back at him and her gaze settled on his mouth for a beat too long. Blood rushed in his ears. When she realised her preoccupation she jerked away.

'I didn't think you knew your own mind.' She swallowed. 'That wasn't fair of me. I'm sorry for doubting you. And I'm sorry I haven't been more supportive of your decision.'

'Hell, don't apologise.' Coffee sloshed over the side of his mug and he mopped it up with the sleeve of his shirt. 'I needed your challenges to make me analyse what I was doing and what it is I want. I should be thanking you for forcing me to face facts.' For forcing him to grow up.

When he glanced back up he found her making a detailed inventory of his chest and shoulders. Her lips parted and fire licked along his veins.

Don't betray yourself, he tutored himself. *Don't!*

Her eyes searched his, and then the light in them dulled and she glanced away, biting her lip.

He had to close his eyes. 'You don't need to apologise about anything.'

He opened his eyes and almost groaned at the strain in her face. He made himself grin, wanting to wipe the tension away, wanting desperately for things to return to normal between them again.

'Though I have to say if I'd known that calling you on the way you've been treating me would change your thinking I'd have done it days ago.'

'Oh, it wasn't that.' She offered him a weak smile that didn't reach her eyes. 'It was watching you with Laura and Lochie last Saturday.'

He'd sensed that had been a test. He just hadn't known if he'd passed it or not.

'I had a ball.'

'I know. And so did they.'

'They're great kids.'

Just for a moment her eyes danced. 'Laura can be a challenge at times.'

'She just needs to loosen up a bit, that's all.' In the same way Meg needed to loosen up.

Who made sure Meg had fun these days? Who made sure she didn't take herself too seriously? She'd said that the baby gave her joy, but it wasn't here yet. What else gave her joy? It seemed to him that at the moment Meg was too busy for joy, and that was no way to live a life.

He'd need to ponder that a bit more, but in the meantime…

'What's your beef with the car?'

That brought the life back to her cheeks. He sat back, intrigued.

'Could you have picked a more boring car if you'd tried?'

'*You* have a station wagon,' he pointed out.

'But at least mine is a sporty version and it's useful for work. And it's blue!'

'The colour doesn't matter.'

'Of course it does.' She leant to towards him. 'I understand you want to prove you're good father material, but that doesn't mean you have to become *beige*!'

'Beige' had been their teenage term for all things boring.

'I agree that with a baby you'll need a car. But you're allowed to buy a car you'll enjoy. A two-seat convertible may not be practical, but you're an action man, Ben, and you like speed. You could've bought some powerful V6 thing that you could open up on the freeway, or a four-wheel drive you could take off-road and drive on the beach—or anything other than that boring beige box sitting in my driveway.'

He considered her words.

'Do you think fatherhood is going to be beige?' she demanded.

'No!'

She closed her eyes and let out a breath. 'That's something, at least.'

He saw it then—the reason for her outburst. She'd started to believe in him, in his sense of purpose and determination, and then he'd turned up in that most conservative of conservative cars and he'd freaked her out.

Again.

He was determined to get things back on an even footing between them again. And he'd succeed. As long as he ignored the sweet temptation of her lips and the long clean line of her limbs. And the desire that flared in her green-flecked eyes.

'You don't have to change who you are, Ben. You might not be travelling around the globe any more, throwing yourself off mountains, negotiating the rapids of some huge river or trekking to base camp at Everest—but, for heaven's sake, it doesn't mean you have to give up your motorbike, does it?'

That—trading in his bike—had been darn hard. It was why it had taken him a full month of being back in Fingal Bay before he'd found the courage to do it. But he'd figured it was a symbol of his old life and therefore had to go. But if Meg was right…

'I want you to go back to that stupid car yard and buy it back.'

A weight lifted from his shoulders. He opened and closed his hands. 'You think I should?'

'Yes! Where else am I going to get my occasional pillion-passenger thrill? All that speed and power? And, while I know you can't literally feel the wind in your hair because of the helmet, that's exactly what it feels like. It's like flying.'

He had a vision of Meg on the back of his bike, her front pressed against his back and her arms wrapped around his waist. He shot to his feet. 'If I race back now I might catch the manager before he leaves for the day.' He had to get his bike back. 'He had a nice-looking four wheel drive in stock. That could be a bit of fun.' He rubbed at his jaw. 'I could take it for a test drive.'

Meg trailed after him to the front door. 'Good luck.'

Halfway down the path, he swung back. 'What are you doing Saturday?'

'Elsie and I are shopping for wedding outfits in the morning.' She grimaced. 'It's not like we've left it to the last minute or anything, but that grandmother of yours can be darn slippery when she wants to be.'

The wedding was a fortnight this Saturday. 'And in the afternoon?'

She shook her head and shrugged.

'Keep it free,' he ordered. Then he strode back, slipped a hand around the back of her head and pressed a kiss to her brow. 'Thanks, Meg.'

And then he left before he did something stupid, like kiss her for real. That wouldn't be getting their friendship back on track.

Meg glanced up at the tap on the back door. 'How did the shopping go?' Ben asked, stepping into the family room with the kind of grin designed to bring a grown woman to her knees.

Her heart swelled at the sight of him. *Don't drool. Smile. Don't forget to smile.*

The smiling was easy. Holding back a groan of pure need wasn't. 'The shopping? Oh, it went surprisingly well,' she managed. Elsie had been remarkably amiable and co-operative. 'We both now have outfits.'

They'd found a lovely lavender suit in shot silk for Elsie. Though she'd protested that it was too young for her, her protests had subsided once Meg had pronounced it perfect. Meg had settled on a deep purple satin halter dress with a chiffon overlay that hid her growing baby bulge. It made her feel like a princess.

'How are the wedding preparation coming along? What do you need me to do this week?'

Ben had, without murmur, executed to perfection whatever job she'd assigned to him. He'd been amazing.

She thought of the request she'd made of Dave and bit her lip. Perhaps she should call that off. Ben had settled into a routine here as if…almost as if he'd never been away. The thought of him leaving…

She shook herself. The wedding. They were talking about the wedding. 'You have a suit?'

'Yep.'

'Then there's not much else to be done. The marquee is being erected on the Friday afternoon prior, and the tables and chairs will all be set up then too.'

'I'll make sure I'm here in case there are any hitches.'

'Thank you.' He eyed her for a moment. It made her skin prickle. 'What?'

He shook himself. 'Have you managed to keep this afternoon free?'

'Uh-huh.' Something in her stomach shifted—a dark, dangerous thrill at the thought of spending a whole afternoon in Ben's company. 'What do you have planned?' If both of them were sensible it would be something practical and beige boring.

Ben's eyes—the way they danced and the way that grin hooked up the right side of his face—told her this afternoon's adventure, whatever it might be, was not going to be beige.

'It's a surprise.'

Her blood quickened. She should make an excuse and cry off, but…

Damn it all, this was Ben—*her best friend*—and that grin of his was irresistible. She glanced down at her sundress. 'Is what I'm wearing okay?'

'Absolutely not.' His grin widened. 'You're going to need a pair of swimmers, and something to put on over them to protect you from sunburn.'

Her bones heated up. She really, truly should make an excuse. 'And a hat, I suppose?' she said, moving in the direction of her bedroom to change.

'You get the picture,' he said.

Meg lifted her face into the breeze and let out a yell for the sheer fun of it. Ben had driven them into Nelson Bay in his brand new *red* four-wheel drive to hire a rubber dinghy with an outboard motor for the afternoon. They were zipping across the vast expanse of the bay as if they were flying.

Ben had given her the wind in her hair for real, and she couldn't remember the last time she'd had this much fun. She released the rope that ran around the dinghy's perimeter and flung her arms back, giving herself up to sheer exhilaration.

'Meg!'

She opened her eyes at Ben's shout, saw they were about to hit the wake from a speedboat, and grabbed the rope again for balance. They bounced over the waves, her knees cushioned by the buoyant softness of the rubber base.

Eventually Ben cut the motor and they drifted. She trailed her hand in the water, relishing its refreshing coolness as she dragged the scent of salt and summer into her lungs. Silver scales glittered in the sun when a fish jumped out of the water nearby. Three pelicans watched from a few metres away, and above them a flock of seagulls cried as they headed for the marina.

The pelicans set off after them, and Meg turned around and stretched her legs out. The dinghy was only small, but there was plenty of room for

Meg and Ben to sit facing one another, with their legs stretched to the side. She savoured the way the dinghy rocked and swayed, making their legs press against each other's, the warm surge that shot through her at each contact.

Ever since that kiss she'd found herself craving to touch Ben—to test the firmness of his skin, to explore his muscled leanness and discover if it would unleash the heat that could rise in her without any warning.

It was dangerous, touching like this, but she couldn't stop herself. Besides, it was summer—the sun shone, the gulls wheeled and screeched, and water splashed against the sides of the dingy. For a moment it all made her feel young and reckless.

'This was a brilliant idea, Ben.'

He grinned. 'It's certainly had the desired effect.'

She reached up to adjust the brim of her sunhat. 'Which was?'

'To put the colour back in your cheeks.'

She stilled. It was strange to have someone looking out for her, looking after her. 'Thank you.' If Ben did stay—

She cut that thought off. Whether Ben stayed or not, it wasn't his job to look after her. He might fill her with heat, but that didn't mean they had any kind of future together.

Except as friends.

He shrugged. 'Besides, it's nice to have some buddy-time.'

She gritted her teeth. Buddy-time was excellent. It *was*!

She glanced at him and tried to decipher the emotions that tangled inside her, coiling her up tight.

She started to name them silently. One: desire. Her lips twisted. *Please God, let that pass.* Two: anger that he'd turned her nicely ordered world on its head. She shook her head. *Deal with it.* Three: love for her oldest, dearest friend, for all they'd been through together, for all they'd shared, and for all the support and friendship he'd given her over the years.

And there was another emotion there too— something that burned and chafed. A throbbing sore. It was...

Hurt.

That made her blink. Hurt? She swallowed and forced herself to examine the feeling. An ache started at her temples. Hurt that he'd stay in Port

Stephens for their baby in a way he'd never have stayed for her.

Oh, that was petty. And nonsensical.

She rubbed her hands up and down her arms. She hadn't harboured hidden hopes that Ben would come back for her. *She hadn't!* But seeing him now on such a regular basis...not to mention that kiss on the beach...that devastating kiss...

'Cold?'

She shook her head and abruptly dropped her hands back to her lap. She dragged in a breath. She had to be careful. She couldn't go weaving Ben into her romantic fantasies. It would end in tears. It would wreck their friendship. And that would be the worst thing in the world. It was why she hadn't let herself get hooked on that kiss ten years ago. It was why she had to forget that kiss the other night.

A romantic relationship—even if Ben was willing—wasn't worth risking their friendship over.

Deep inside, a part of her started to weep. She swallowed. Hormones, that was all.

'I can still hardly believe that Elsie and your father are marrying.'

She nodded, prayed her voice would work properly, prayed she could hide her strain. 'It shows a remarkable optimism on both their parts.'

He surveyed her for a moment. 'How are you getting on with your father?'

'Same as usual.' She lifted her face to the sun to counter a sudden chill. 'Neither he nor Elsie have mentioned my outburst. It seems we're all back to pretending it never happened.' Not that she knew what else she'd been expecting. Or hoping for. 'It's the elephant in the room nobody mentions.'

'It's had a good effect on Elsie, though.'

She straightened from her slouch. 'No?'

'Yep.' He flicked water at her. 'She's less buttoned-up and more relaxed. She makes more of an effort at conversation too.'

'No?'

He flicked water at her again. 'Yep.'

'I'd say that's down to the effect of her romance with my father.'

'She's even knitting the baby some booties.'

Meg leant towards him, even though she was in danger of getting more water flicked at her. 'You're kidding me?'

He didn't flick more water at her, but she realised it had been a mistake to lean towards him when the scent of leather and whisky slugged into her, heating her up…tightening her up. Making her want forbidden things.

She sat back. Darn it all! How on earth could she be so aware of his scent out here in the vast expanse of the bay? Surely the salt water and the sun should erase it, dilute it?

She scooped up a whole handful of water and threw it at him.

And then they had the kind of water fight that drenched them both and had her squealing and him laughing and them both breathing heavily from the exertion.

'How long since you've been out on the bay like this?' he demanded, subsiding back into his corner.

'Like this?' She readjusted her sunhat. 'Probably not since the last time we did it.'

'That has to be two years ago!'

'I've been out on a couple of dinner cruises, and I've swum more times than I can count.'

'What about kayaking?'

That was one of her favourite things—to take a kayak out in the early evening, when the shadows were long, the light dusky and the water calm. Paddling around the bay left her feeling at one with nature and the world. But when had she'd actually last done that?

She cocked her head to one side. She'd gone out a few times in December, but...

She hadn't been out once this year! 'I...I guess I've been busy.'

'You need to stop and smell the roses.'

He was right. This afternoon—full of sun, bay and a beat-up rubber dinghy—had proved that to her. She wanted to set her child a good example. She had no intention of turning into a distracted workaholic mother. She thought about her father and Elsie, how easily they'd fallen into unhealthy routines and habits.

She swallowed and glanced at Ben. He always took the time to smell the roses. Her lips twisted. Sometimes he breathed them in a little too deeply, and for a little too long, but nobody could accuse him of not living life to the full.

Would he still feel life was full after he'd been living in Port Stephens for a couple of years?

She glanced around. It was beautiful here. He was having fun, wasn't he?

For today.

But what would happen tomorrow, the day after that, and next week, next month, or even next year? *Please, God, don't let Ben be miserable.*

There was still so much that had to be settled.

She leant back and swallowed. 'I agree it's important to slow down and to enjoy all the best that life
has to offer, but you've still got some big decisions
ahead of you, Ben.' And she doubted she'd be able
to relax fully until he'd made them.

'Like?'

'Like what are you going to do with Elsie's
house? Will you live there on your own after the
wedding?'

'I haven't thought about it.'

'And what about a job? I'm not meaning to be
nosy or pushy or anything, but…'

His lips twitched. 'But?'

'I figure you don't want to live off your savings
for ever.'

'I have a couple of irons in the fire.'

He did? She opened her mouth but he held up a
hand to forestall her.

'Once I have something concrete to report you'll
be the first to know. I promise.'

She wanted to demand a timeframe on his promise, but she knew he'd scoff at that. And probably
rightly so.

'Do you think I should move into Elsie's house?'

Her mouth dried. 'I…'

'If I do, I'll be paying her rent.' He scowled.

'I don't want her to give the darn thing to me. It's hers.'

She eyed him for a moment. 'What if she gifts it to the baby?'

His mouth opened and closed but no sound came out. It obviously wasn't a scenario he'd envisaged. 'I...' He didn't go on.

She glanced away, her stomach shrinking. The two of them had to have a serious conversation. But not today. They could save it for some other time.

'You better spit it out, Meg.'

She glared at the water. Ben knowing her so well could be darn inconvenient at times. She blew out a breath and turned to him. 'There are a few things I think we need to discuss in relation to the baby, but they can wait until after the wedding. It's such a glorious afternoon.'

And she didn't want to spoil it. Or ruin this easy-going camaraderie that should have been familiar to them but had been elusive these last few weeks.

'It could be the perfect afternoon for such a discussion,' he countered, gesturing to the sun, the bay and the holiday atmosphere of these last dog days of summer. 'When we're both relaxed.'

If she uttered the C-word he wouldn't remain relaxed. Still, she knew him well enough to know he wouldn't let it drop. She glanced around. Maybe he was right. Maybe she *should* lay a few things out there for him to mull over before Dave presented him with that dream offer. It only seemed fair.

She shivered, suddenly chilled, as if a cloud had passed over the sun. 'You won't like it,' she warned.

'I'm a big boy, Meg. I have broad shoulders.'

'You want to know if I think you should live in Elsie's house? That depends on…' She swallowed.

'On?'

'On what kind of access you want to have to the baby.'

He frowned. 'What do you mean?'

She wasn't going to be able to get away with not using the C-word. Dancing around it would only make matters worse.

'What I'm talking about, Ben, are our custody arrangements.'

Custody?

Ben flinched as the word ripped beneath his guard. His head was filled with the sound of shouting and screaming and abuse.

Custody?

'No!' He stabbed a finger at her. He swore. Once. Hard. Tried to quieten the racket in his head. He swore again, the storm raging inside him growing in strength. 'What the bloody hell are you talking about? *Custody?*' He spat the word out. 'No way! We don't need *custody* arrangements. We aren't like that. You and I can work it out like civilised people.'

Meg had gone white.

He realised he was shouting. Just like his mother had shouted. Just like his father had shouted. He couldn't stop. 'We're supposed to be friends.'

She swallowed and bile filled his mouth. Was she afraid of him? Wind rushed through his ears. No! She knew him well enough to know he'd never hut her. Didn't she?

His hands clenched. If she knew him well enough, she'd have never raised this issue in the first place.

'We're friends who are having a baby,' she said, her voice low. 'We need certain safeguards in place to ensure—'

'Garbage!' He slashed a hand through the air. 'We can keep going the way we have been—the way we've always done things. When you've had the baby I can come over any time and help, maybe take care of it some days while you're at work, and help you in the evenings with feeding and baths and—'

'So basically we'd live like a married couple but without the benefits?'

Her scorn almost blasted the flesh from his bones.

'No, Ben, that's *not* how it's going to be. Living like that—don't you think it would do our child's head in?' She stabbed a finger at him. 'Besides, I still believe in love and marriage. I am *so* not going to have you cramp my style like that.'

The storm inside him built to fever-pitch. 'You really mean to let another man help raise *my* child?'

'That's something you're going to have to learn to live with. Just like I will if you ever become serious about a woman.'

He went ice-cold then. 'You never wanted me as part of this picture, did you? I've ruined your pretty fantasy of domestic bliss and now you're trying to punish me.' He leaned towards her. 'You're hoping this will drive me away.'

The last of the colour bled from her face. 'That's not true.'

Wasn't it? His harsh laugh told her better than words could what he thought about that.

Her colour didn't return. She gripped her hands together in her lap. 'I want you to decide what you want the custody arrangements to be. Do you want fifty-fifty custody? A night through the week and every second weekend? Or…whatever? This is something we need to settle.'

Custody. The word stabbed through him, leaving a great gaping hole at the centre of his being. He wanted to cover his ears and hide under his bed as he had as a ten-year-old. The sense of helplessness, of his life spinning out of control, made him suddenly ferocious.

'What if I want full custody?' he snarled.

He wanted to frighten her. He wanted her to back down, to admit that this was all a mistake, that she was sorry and she didn't mean it.

He wanted her to acknowledge that he wasn't like his father!

Her chin shot up. 'You wouldn't get it.'

A savage laugh ripped from his throat. He should have known better. Meg would be well versed in her rights. She'd have made sure of them before bringing this subject up.

'I want the custody arrangements settled in black and white before the baby is born.'

That ice-cold remoteness settled over him again.

She didn't trust him. 'Do you have to live your entire life by rules?'

Her throat bobbed as she swallowed. 'I'm sorry, Ben, but in this instance I'm going to choose what's best for the baby, not what's best for you.'

She was choosing what was best for *her*. End of story. Acid burned his throat. Meg didn't even know who he was any more, and he sure as hell didn't know her. The pedestal he'd had her on for all these years had toppled and smashed.

'And as for you living next door in Elsie's house...' She shook her head. 'I think that's a very bad idea.'

He didn't say another word. He just started the dinghy's motor and headed for shore.

'How's Meg?'

Ben scowled as he reached for a beer. With a muttered oath he put it back and chose a can of lemon squash instead. He swung back to Elsie, the habit of a lifetime's loyalty preventing him from saying what he wanted to say—from howling out his rage.

'She's fine.'

Elsie sat at the kitchen table, knitting. It reminded him of Meg's baby shawl, and the almost completed crib he'd been working on in Elsie's garden shed.

'Is she okay with me taking her mother's place?'

Whoa! He reached out a hand to steady himself against the counter. Where on earth had that come from? He shook his head and counted to three. 'Let's get a couple of things straight. First of all, you won't be taking her mother's place. Meg is all grown-up.'

She might be grown-up, but she was also pedantic, anal and cruel.

He hauled in a breath. 'She doesn't need a mother any more. For heaven's sake, she's going to be a mother herself soon.'

He added controlling, jealous and possessive to his list. He adjusted his stance.

'Secondly, she won't be doing anything daft like calling you Mum.'

Elsie stared back at him. 'I meant taking her mother's place in her father's affections,' she finally said.

Oh. He frowned.

'Do you think she minds us marrying?'

Meg might be a lot of things he hadn't counted on, but she wasn't petty. 'She's throwing you a wedding. Doesn't that say it all?'

Elsie paused in her knitting. 'The thing is, she always was the kind of girl to put on a brave front.' She tapped a knitting needle against the table. 'You both were.'

He pulled out a chair and sat before he fell.

'Do *you* mind Laurie and I marrying?'

He shook his head. 'No.' And he realised he meant it.

'Good.' She nodded. 'Yes, that's good.' She stared at him for a bit, and then leaned towards him a fraction. 'Do you think Meg will let the baby call me Grandma?'

He didn't know what to say. 'I expect so. If that's what you want. You'll have to tell her that's what you'd prefer, though, rather than Elsie,' he couldn't resist adding.

Elsie set her knitting down. She took off her glasses and rubbed her eyes. Finally she looked at him again. 'After she left, I never heard from your mother, Ben. Not once.'

Ben's mouth went dry.

Elsie's hands shook. 'I waited and waited.'

Just for a moment the room, the table and Elsie receded. And then they came rushing back. 'But…?' he croaked.

Elsie shook her head, looking suddenly old.

'But…nothing. I can't tell you anything, though I wish to heaven I could. I don't know where she went. I don't know if she's alive or not. All I do know is it's been eighteen years.' A breath shuddered out of her. 'And that she knows how to get in contact with us, but to the best of my knowledge she's never tried to.'

He stared at her, trying to process what she'd said and how he felt about it.

'Your father broke something in her.'

He shook his head at that. 'No. The way they acted—they let hate and bitterness destroy them. She had a chance to pull back. They both did. But they chose not to. She was as much to blame as him.'

Elsie clenched her hand. 'All I know is that she left and I grieved. My only child…'

Ben thought about the child Meg carried and closed his eyes.

'When I came out of that fog I…we…me and you were set in our ways, our routines, our way of dealing with each other.'

Was it that simple? Elsie had been grief-stricken and just hadn't known how to deal with a young boy whose whole world had imploded.

'Your mother always said I suffocated her and

that's why she went with your father. I failed her somehow—I still don't know how, can't find any explanation for it—and I just didn't want to go through all that again.'

He pulled in a breath. 'So you kept me at arm's length?'

'It was wrong of me, Ben, and I'm sorry.'

So much pain and misery. If his and Meg's child ever disappeared the way his mother had, could he honestly say he'd deal with it any better than Elsie had? He didn't know.

In the end he swallowed and nodded. 'Thank you for explaining it to me.'

'It was long overdue.'

He didn't know what to do, what to say.

'I'm grateful you had Meg.'

Meg. Her name burned through him. What would Meg want him to do now?

From somewhere he found a smile, and it didn't feel forced. 'I'm sure she'll be happy for the baby to call you Grandma.'

CHAPTER TEN

ON THE MORNING of the wedding Meg woke early. She leapt out of bed, pulled on a robe and raced downstairs, her mind throbbing with the million things that must need doing. And then she pulled to a halt in the kitchen and turned on the spot. Actually, what *was* there to do? Everything was pretty much done. She and Elsie had hair and make-up appointments later in the day, and her father was coming over mid-afternoon to get ready for the wedding, but till then her time was her own.

She made a cup of tea and let herself out through the glass sliding door. The garden looked lovely, and the marquee sat in the midst of it like a joyful jewel.

And then she saw Ben.

He stood a few feet away, a steaming mug of his own in hand, surveying the marquee too. He looked deliciously dishevelled and rumpled, as if he'd only just climbed out of bed. He didn't do designer stubble. Ben didn't do designer anything. There was nothing designed in the way he looked, but...

Her hand tightened about her mug. An ache burned in her abdomen. She'd barely seen him these last two weeks. He'd rung a few times, to check if there was anything she'd needed him to do, but he'd kept the calls brief and businesslike. He'd overseen the assembly of the marquee yesterday afternoon, but he'd disappeared back next door as soon as the workmen had left. He'd avoided her ever since she'd mentioned the C word.

'Morning, Meg.'

He didn't turn his head to look at her now either.

A cold fist closed about her heart. He was her best friend. He'd been an integral part of her life for eighteen years. She couldn't lose him. If she lost his friendship she would lose a part of herself.

The same way her father had lost a part of himself the day her mother had died.

The pressure in her chest grew until she thought it might split her in two.

'Lovely day for a wedding.'

He was talking to her about the weather. Everything in the garden blurred. She lifted her face to the sky and blinked, tried to draw breath into lungs that had cramped.

When she didn't speak, he turned to look at her. His eyes darkened and his face paled at whatever he saw in her face.

He shook his head. 'Don't look at me like that.'

She couldn't help it. 'Do you mean to resent me for ever? Do you mean to keep avoiding me? All because I want to do what's right for our baby?' The words tumbled out, tripping and falling over each other. 'Don't you trust me any more, Ben?'

His head snapped back. 'This is about your trust, not mine!' He stabbed a finger at her. 'You wouldn't need some third party to come in and organise custody arrangements if you trusted me.'

She flinched, but she held her ground. 'Have you considered the fact that it might be myself I don't trust?' She poured the rest of her now tepid tea onto the nearest rosebush. 'I already feel crazily possessive about this baby.'

She rested a hand against her rounded stomach. He followed the movement. She moistened her lips when he met her gaze again. 'I'm going to find it hard to share this child with anyone—even with you, Ben. It wasn't part of my grand plan.' As he well knew. 'I know that's far from noble, but I can't help the way I feel. I also know that you're this baby's father and you have a right to be a part of its life.'

But the first time their baby spent twenty-four full hours with Ben—twenty-four hours away from her—she'd cry her eyes out. She'd wander from room to room in her huge house, lost.

'Having everything down in black and white will protect your rights. Have you not considered that?'

One glance at his face told her he hadn't.

'I don't see why making everything clear—what we expect from each other and what our child can expect from us—is such a bad thing.'

He didn't say anything. He didn't even move.

'I understand that down the track things might change. We can discuss and adapt to those changes as and when we need to. I'm not locking us into a for ever contract. We can include a clause that says we'll renegotiate every two years, if you want.'

But she knew they needed something on paper that would set out their responsibilities and expectations and how they'd move forward.

For the sake of the baby.

And for the sake of their friendship.

'I know you love this baby, Ben.'

Dark eyes surveyed her.

'You wouldn't turn your whole life on its head for no good reason. You want to be a good father.'

He'd stay for the baby in a way he'd never have stayed for her, but she wanted him to stay. She wanted it so badly she could almost taste it.

'And you think agreeing to legalise our custody arrangements will prove I'll be a good father?'

She tried not to flinch at the scorn in his voice. She was asking him to face his greatest fear. Nobody did that without putting up a fight. And when he wanted to Ben could put up a hell of a fight.

She tipped up her chin. 'It'll make us better co-parents. So, yes—I think it *will* make me a better mother and you a better father.'

His jaw slackened.

She stared at him and then shook her head. Her throat tightened. She'd really started to believe that he'd stay, but now...

'I'm sorry,' she whispered. 'If I'd known five months ago what would come of asking you to be my sperm donor I'd never have asked.' She'd have left well alone and not put him through all this.

He stiffened. 'But I want this baby.'

Something inside her snapped then. 'Well, then, suck it up.' She tossed her mug to the soft grass at her feet and planted her hands on her hips. 'If you want this baby then man up to your responsibilities. If you can't do that—if they intimidate you that much—then run off back to Africa and go bungee-jump off a high bridge, or rappel down a cliff, or go deep-sea diving in the Atlantic, or any of those other things that aren't half as scary as fatherhood!'

He folded his arms and nodded. 'That's better. That meek and mild act doesn't suit you.'

Her hand clenched. She stared at her fist and then at his jaw.

'You're right. I do need to man up and face my responsibilities.'

Her hand promptly unclenched.

He ran a hand through his hair. 'Especially when they intimidate me, I expect.'

She stared, and then shook herself. 'Exactly at what point in the conversation did you come to that conclusion?'

'When you said how possessive you feel about the baby.'

Her nose started to curl. 'When you realised a custody agreement would protect your interests?'

'When I realised you weren't my mother.'

Everything inside her stilled.

'When I realised that, regardless of what happens, you will *never* become my mother. I know you will always put the baby's best interests first. That's when I realised I was fighting shadows—because regardless of what differences we might have in the future, Meg, we will never re-enact my parents' drama.'

She folded her arms.

'Are you going to tell me off now, for taking so long to come to that conclusion?'

'I'm going to tell you off for not telling me you'd already come to that conclusion. For letting me rabbit on and...' And abuse him.

'I needed a few moments to process the discovery.' He shifted his weight. 'And I wanted to razz you a bit until you stopped looking so damn fragile and depressed. That's not like you, Meg. What the hell is that all about?'

She glanced away.

'I want the truth.'

That made her smile. 'Have we ever been less than honest with each other?' They knew each other too well to lie effectively to the other. 'I've been feeling sick this past fortnight, worried that

I've hurt our friendship. I want to do what's right for the baby. But hurting you kills me.'

He tossed his now-empty mug to the grass, as she had earlier. It rolled towards her mug, the two handles almost touching. At his sides, his hands clenched.

'The thing is, Ben, after this baby your friendship is the most important thing in the world to me. If I lost it...'

With a smothered oath, he closed the distance between them and pulled her in close, hugged her tightly. 'That's not going to happen, Meg. It will never happen.'

He held her tight, and yet she felt as if she was falling and falling without an end in sight. Even first thing in the morning he smelled of leather and whisky. She tried to focus on that instead of falling.

Eventually she disengaged herself. 'There's something else that's been bothering me.'

'What's that?'

'You keep saying you have no intention of forming a serious relationship with any woman.'

'I don't.'

'Well, I think you need to seriously rethink

that philosophy of yours, because quite frankly it sucks.'

He gaped at her.

'You think fatherhood will be fulfilling, don't you?'

'Yes, but—'

'So can committing to one person and building a life with them.'

He glared. 'For you, perhaps.'

'And for you too. You're not exempt from the rest of the human race. No matter how much you'd like to think you are.'

He adjusted his stance, slammed his hands to his hips. 'What is it with you? You've never tried to change my mind on this before.'

That was true, but… 'I never thought you'd want fatherhood either, but I was obviously wrong about that. And I think *you're* wrong to discount a long-term romantic relationship.'

He shook his head. 'I'm not risking it.'

'You just admitted I'm not like your mother. There are other women—' the words tasted like acid on her tongue but she forced them out '— who aren't like your mother either.' She'd hate to see him with another woman, which didn't make a whole lot of sense. She closed her mind to the pictures that bombarded her.

'But I know you, Meg. I've known you for most of my life.'

'Then take the time to get to know someone else.'

His face shuttered closed. 'No.'

She refused to give up. 'I think you'll be a brilliant father. I think you deserve to have lots more children. Wouldn't you like that?'

He didn't say anything, and she couldn't read his face.

'I think you'd make a wonderful husband too.' She could see it more clearly than she'd ever thought possible and it made her heart beat harder and faster. 'I think any woman would be lucky to have you in her life. And, Ben, I think it would make you happy.' And she wanted him happy with every fibre of her being.

He thrust out his jaw. 'I'm perfectly happy as I am.'

She wanted to call him a liar, except...

Except maybe he was right. The beguiling picture of Ben as a loving husband and doting father faded. Maybe the things that would make her happy would only make him miserable. The thought cut at her with a ferocity she couldn't account for.

She swallowed. 'I just want you to be happy,' she whispered.

He blew out a breath. 'I know.'

She wanted Ben to stay in Port Stephens. She *really* wanted that. If he fell in love with some woman... She shied away from the thought.

Her heart burned. She twisted her hands together. This evening Dave meant to offer Ben the chance to fulfil his dream—to offer him a place on that yacht.

'Can I hit you with another scary proposition?'

He squared his shoulders. 'You bet.'

Would it translate into emotional blackmail? Was it an attempt to make sure he did stay?

He leant down to peer into her face. 'Meg?'

She shook herself. It wasn't blackmail. It was her making sure Ben had all the options, knew his choices, that was all.

She swallowed. 'Would you like to be my birth partner? Would you like to be present at the birth of our child?'

He stilled.

'If you want to think about it—'

'I don't need to think about it.' Wonder filled his face. 'Yes, Meg. Yes. A thousand times yes.'

Finally she found she could smile again. What was a round-the-world yacht voyage compared to seeing his own child born? Behind her back, she crossed her fingers.

'Megan, I'm marrying Elsie because I care about her.' Laurie Parrish lifted his chin. 'Because I love her.'

Meg glanced up from fussing with her dress. In ten minutes he and she would walk out into the garden to meet Elsie and Ben and the ceremony would begin.

'I never doubted it for a moment.' She hesitated, and then leant across and took the liberty of straightening his tie.

He took her hand before she could move away again. 'Before I embark on my new life I want to apologise to you and acknowledge that I haven't been much of a father to you. I can't…' His voice grew gruff. 'I can't tell you how much I regret that.'

She stared at him and finally nodded. It was why he'd given her the house. She'd always sensed that.

But it was nice to hear him acknowledge it out loud too. 'Okay, Dad, apology accepted.'

She tried to disengage her hand, but he refused to release it. 'I'm also aware that an apology and an expression of regret doesn't mean that we're suddenly going to have a great relationship.'

She blinked. *Wow!*

'But if it would be okay with you, if it won't make you uncomfortable or unhappy, I would like to try and build a relationship—a good, solid relationship—with you.'

Her initial scepticism turned to all-out shock.

'Would you have a problem with that?'

Slowly, she shook her head. She had absolutely no problem with that. It would be wonderful for her child to have grandparents who loved it, who wanted to be involved. Only…

She straightened. 'I'll need you to be a bit more enthusiastic and engaged. Not just in my life but in your own too.' She would need him to make some of the running instead of leaving it all up to her. But if he truly meant it…

Her heart lifted and the resentment that had built inside her these last few months started to abate. Unlike Ben, bitterness and anger hadn't crippled her during her teenage years. Sadness and yearning had. She couldn't erase that sadness and yearning now, and nor could her father. Nobody could. They would never get back those lost years, but she was willing to put effort into the future.

'Giving me the house was your way of saying sorry and trying to make amends, wasn't it?'

He nodded. 'I wanted your future secure. It seemed the least I could do.'

His admission touched her.

'But moving out of this house brought me to my senses about Elsie too. Missing her made me realise what she'd come to mean to me.'

So that had been the trigger—an illness, a recuperation, and then a change of address. Evidently romance worked in mysterious ways.

'I know this isn't going to change anything, Megan, but when you were growing up I thought you were spending so much time at Elsie's because she'd become a kind of surrogate mother to you. When I was recovering from my illness and Elsie was coming over to sit with me, I found out she'd thought Ben was spending that time here because I was providing the role of surrogate father. With each of us thinking that...' He pressed his fingers to his eyes. 'We just let things slide along the way they were.'

If they'd known differently, would he and Elsie have roused themselves from their depression? It was something they'd never know now.

She squeezed his hand. 'I think it's time to put the past behind us.' And as she said the words she realised she meant them. She had a baby on the way. She wanted to look towards the future, not back to the past.

'C'mon, I think it's time.'

'Is Ben going to do the right thing by you and the baby?'

She and Ben hadn't told a soul that he was the baby's father. But her father and Elsie weren't stupid or blind. She pulled in a breath. 'Yes, he will. He always does what's best for me.'

She just wished she knew if that meant he was staying or if he was going. 'You have to understand, though, that what you think is best and what Ben and I think is best may be two very different things.' She didn't want the older couple hassling Ben, pressuring him.

'I understand.' Her father nodded heavily. 'I have no right to interfere. I just want to see you happy, Megan.'

'No,' she agreed, 'you're *not* allowed to interfere.' She took his arm and squeezed it. 'But you are allowed to care.'

She smiled up at him. He smiled back. 'C'mon—let's go get you married and then celebrate in style.'

The moment Meg stepped into the rose garden with her father Ben couldn't take his eyes from her.

'Are they there yet?' Elsie asked, her voice fretful, her fingers tapping against the kitchen table. 'They're late.'

He snapped to. 'They're exactly on time.' He kept his eyes on Meg for as long as he could as he backed away from the window. Swallowing, he turned to find Elsie alternately plucking at her skirt, her flowers and her hair. It was good to know she wasn't as cool and calm as she appeared or wanted everyone to think. 'Ready?'

She nodded. She looked lovelier than he'd ever seen her. He thought about what Meg would want him to say at this moment. 'Elsie?'

She glanced up at him.

'Mr Parrish is a very lucky man.'

'Oh!' Her cheeks turned pink.

He suddenly grinned. 'I expect he's going to take one look at you and want to drag you away from the celebrations at an indecently early hour.'

Her cheeks turned even redder and she pressed her hands to them. The she reached out and swatted him with her bouquet. 'Don't talk such nonsense, Ben!'

He tucked her hand into the crock of his arm and led her through the house and out through the front door. 'It's not nonsense. Just you wait.'

Ben had meant to watch for the expression on Laurie's face the first moment he glimpsed Elsie, but one sidelong glance at Meg and Ben's attention was lost. Perspiration prickled his nape. He couldn't drag his gaze away.

Meg wore a deep purplish-blue dress, and in the sun it gleamed like a jewel. She stood there erect and proud, with her gently rounded stomach, looking out-of-this-world desirable. Like a Grecian goddess. He stared at her bare shoulders and all he could think of was pressing kisses to the beckoning golden skin. He could imagine their satin sun-kissed warmth. He sucked air into oxygen-starved lungs. A raging thirst built inside him.

A diamante brooch gathered the material of the dress between her breasts. Filmy material floated in the breeze and drifted down to her ankles. She'd be wearing sexy sandals and he wanted to look, really he did, but he found it impossible to drag his gaze from the lush curves of her breasts.

He moistened his lips. His heart thumped against his ribcage. His skin started to burn. Meg's dress did nothing to hide her new curves. Curves he could imagine in intimate detail—their softness, their weight in his hands, the way her nipples would peak under his hungry gaze as they were doing now. He imagined how they'd tauten further as he ran a thumb back and forth across them, the taste of them and their texture as he—

For Pete's sake!

He wrenched his gaze away, his mouth dry. A halfway decent guy did *not* turn his best friend into an object of lust. A halfway decent guy would not let her think even for a single second that there could ever be anything more between them than friendship.

He did his best to keep his gaze averted from all her golden promise, tried to focus on the ceremony. He wasn't equal to the task—not even when Elsie and Laurie surprised everyone by revealing they'd written their own vows. He was too busy concentrating on not staring at Meg, on not lusting after her, to catch what those vows were.

A quick glance at Meg—a super-quick glance—

told him they'd been touching. Her eyes had grown bright with unshed tears, her smile soft, and her lips—

He dragged his gaze away again, his pulse thundering in his ears.

It seemed to take a hundred years, but finally Elsie and Laurie were pronounced husband and wife. And then Laurie kissed Elsie in a way that didn't help the pressure building in Ben's gut. There were cheers and congratulations all round. Four of Meg's girlfriends threw glittery confetti in the air. Gold and silver spangles settled in Meg's hair, on her cheek and shoulders, and one landed on the skin of her chest just above her—

He jerked his gaze heavenward.

Meg broke away from the group surrounding the newlyweds to slip her arm through his. 'We're going to have a ten-minute photoshoot with the photographer, and then it'll be party time.'

There was a photographer? He glanced around. He hadn't captured the way Ben had been ogling Meg, had he? Please, God.

'You scrub up real nice, Ben Sullivan.' She squeezed his arm. 'I don't think I've seen you in a suit since you stepped in to take me to my high school formal when Jason Prior dumped me to partner Rochelle Collins instead.'

He'd stepped in as a friend back then. He needed to find that same frame of mind, that same outlook, quick-smart.

Minus the kiss that had happened that night!

He dragged in a breath.

Don't think about it.

He'd been a sex-starved teenager back then, that's all.

And Meg had been beautiful.

She's more beautiful now.

'But I don't remember you filling out a suit half so well back then.'

He closed his eyes. Not just at her words, but at the husky tone in which they were uttered. The last thing he needed right now was for Meg to start feeling sexy. At least she had an excuse—pregnancy hormones. Him? He was just low life scum.

If he kissed Meg again it wouldn't stop at kisses. They both knew that. But one night would never be enough for Meg. And two nights was one night too many as far as he was concerned.

It would wreck their friendship. He couldn't risk that—not now they had a child to consider.

'You okay?'

He steeled himself and then glanced down. Her brow had creased, her eyes were wary. He swallowed and nodded.

She gestured towards the newlyweds. 'The service was lovely.'

'Yep.'

His tie tightened about his throat. Please God, don't let her ask him anything specific. He couldn't remember a damn thing about the ceremony.

She smiled, wide and broad. 'I have a good feeling about all of this.'

Just for a moment that made him smile too. 'Pollyanna,' he teased.

Her eyes danced, her lips shone, and hunger stretched through him.

If I lost your friendship, I don't know what I would do.

He swallowed the bile that burned his throat. He couldn't think of anything worse than losing Meg's friendship.

And yet...

He clenched his hands. Yet it wasn't enough to dampen his rising desire to seduce her.

Something in his face must have betrayed him because she snapped away from him, pulling her arm from his. 'Stop looking at me like that!'

The colour had grown high in her cheeks. Her eyes blazed. Neither of those things dampened his libido. That said, he wasn't sure a slap to the face or a cold shower would have much of an effect either.

'Darn it, Ben. I should have known this was how you'd react to the wedding.'

She kept her voice low—bedroom-low—and—

He cut the thought off and tried to focus on her words. 'What are you talking about?'

'All this hearts and flowers stuff has made you want to beat your chest and revert to your usual caveman tactics just to prove you're not affected. That you're immune.'

'Caveman?' he spluttered. 'I'll have you know I have more finesse than that.'

They glared at each other.

'Besides, you're underestimating yourself.' He scowled. 'You look great in that dress.' With a superhuman effort he managed to maintain eye contact and slowly the tension between them lessened. 'Can we get these photos underway?' he growled.

He needed to be away from Meg asap with an ice-cold beer in his hand.

The reception went without a hitch.

The food was great. The music was great. The

company was great. The speech Laurie made thanking Meg and Ben for the wedding and admitting what a lucky man he was, admitting that he'd found a new lease of life, touched even Ben.

The reception went without a hitch except throughout it all Ben was far too aware of Meg. Of the way she moved, the sound of her laughter, the warmth she gave out to all those around her. Of the sultry way she moved on the dance floor. He scowled. She certainly hadn't lacked for dance partners.

He'd made sure that he'd danced too. There were several beautiful women here, and three months ago he'd have done his best to hook up with one of them—go for a drink somewhere and then back to her place afterwards. It seemed like a damn fine plan except…

I don't like the way you treat women.

He'd stopped dancing after that.

His gaze lowered to the rounded curve of Meg's stomach and his throat tightened.

'Hey, buddy!' A clap on the shoulder brought him back.

Ben turned and then stood to shake hands. 'Dave, mate—great to see you here. Meg said you were coming. Have a seat.'

They sat and Dave surveyed him. 'It's been a great night.'

'Yeah.'

'Meg's told me what a help you've been with the wedding prep.'

She had? He shrugged. 'It was nothing.'

Dave glanced at Meg on the dance floor. 'That's not how she sees it.'

He bit back a groan. The last thing he needed was someone admiring Meg when he was doing his damnedest to concentrate on doing anything but.

Dave shifted on his chair to face him more fully. 'Something has popped up in my portfolio that I think will interest you.'

Anything that could keep his mind off Meg for any length of time was a welcome distraction. 'Tell me more.'

'If you want it, I can get you on the crew for a yacht that's setting off around the world. It leaves the week after next and expects to be gone five months.' He shrugged and sat back. 'I know it's something you've always wanted to do.'

Ben stared at the other man and waited for the rush of anticipation to hit him. This was something he'd always wanted—the last challenge on his adventure list. It would kill him to turn it down, but…

He waited and waited.

And kept right on waiting.

The anticipation didn't come. In fact he could barely manage a flicker of interest. He frowned and straightened.

'Mate, I appreciate the offer but…' His eyes sought out Meg on the dance floor, lowered to her baby bump. 'I have bigger fish to fry at the moment.'

Dave shrugged. 'Fair enough. I just wanted to run it by you.'

'And I appreciate it.' But what he wanted and who he was had crystallised in his mind in sharp relief. He was going to be a father and he wanted to be a *good* father—the best.

Dave clapped him on the back. 'I'll catch you later, Ben. It's time to drag that gorgeous wife of mine onto the dance floor.'

Ben waved in absent acknowledgment. A smile grew inside him. He was going to be a father. Nothing could shake him from wanting to be the best one he could be. His new sense of purpose held far more power than his old dreams ever had.

* * *

Her father and Elsie left at a relatively early hour, but the party in Meg's garden continued into the night. She danced with her girlfriends and made sure she spoke to everyone.

Everyone, that was, except Ben.

She stayed away from Ben. Tonight he was just too potent. He wore some gorgeous subtle after-shave that made her think of Omar Sharif and harems, but it didn't completely mask the scent of leather and whisky either, and the combination made her head whirl.

Some instinct warned her that if she gave in to the temptation he represented tonight she'd be lost.

'Meg?' Dave touched her arm and she blinked herself back inside the marquee. 'Winnie and I are heading off, but thanks for a great party. We had a ball.'

'I'm glad you enjoyed yourselves. I'll see you out.'

'No need.'

'Believe me, the fresh air will do me good.'

Keeping busy was the answer. Not remembering the way Ben's eyes had practically devoured her earlier was key too. She swallowed. When he looked at her the way a man looked at a woman he found desirable he skyrocketed her temperature and had her pulse racing off the chart. He made her want to do wild reckless things.

She couldn't do wild and reckless things. She was about to become a mother.

And when he didn't look at her like that, when he gazed at her baby bump with his heart in his eyes—oh, it made her wish for other things. It made her wish they could be a family—a proper family.

But of course that way madness lay. And a broken heart.

She led Dave and Winnie through the rose garden, concentrating on keeping both her temperature and her pulse at even, moderate levels.

Just before they reached the front yard Dave said, 'I made Ben that offer you and I spoke about a while back.'

She stumbled to a halt. Her heart lurched. She had to lock her knees to stop herself from dropping to the ground. 'And...?' Her heart beat against her ribs.

'And I turned it down,' a voice drawled from behind her.

She swung around. *Ben!* And the way his eyes glittered dangerously in the moonlight told her he was less than impressed. She swallowed. In fact he looked downright furious.

'Have I caused any trouble?' Dave murmured.

'Not at all,' she denied, unable to keep the strain from her voice.

Winnie took her husband's arm. 'Thank you both for a lovely evening.' With a quick goodnight, the other couple beat a hasty retreat.

Meg swallowed and turned back to Ben. 'I...'

He raised an eyebrow and folded his arms. 'You can explain, right?'

Could she?

'Another test?' he spat out.

She nodded.

'My word wasn't good enough?'

It should've been, but...' She moistened suddenly parched lips. 'I wanted a guarantee,' she whispered.

He stabbed a finger at her. 'You of all people should know there's no such thing.'

Her heart beat like a panicked animal when he wheeled away from her. 'Please, Ben—'

He swung back. 'What exactly are you most afraid of, Meg? That I'll leave or that I'll stay?'

Then it hit her.

'Oh!'

She took a step away from him. The lock on her knees gave out and she plumped down to the soft grass in a tangle of satin and chiffon. She covered her mouth with one hand as she stared up at him.

Leaving. She was afraid of him leaving. Deathly afraid. Deep-down-in-her-bones afraid.

Break-her-heart afraid.

Because she'd gone and done the unthinkable—she'd fallen in love with Ben.

She'd fallen in love with her best friend. A man who didn't believe in love and marriage or commitment to any woman. She'd fallen in love with him and she didn't want him to leave. And yet by staying he would break her heart afresh every single day of her life to come.

And she would have to bear it.

Because Ben staying was what would be best for their baby.

CHAPTER ELEVEN

WITH HER DRESS mushroomed around her, her hair done up in a pretty knot and her golden shoulders drooping, Meg reminded Ben of a delicate orchid he'd once seen in a rainforest far from civilisation.

He swooped down and drew her back to her feet, his heart clenching at her expression. 'Don't look like that, Meg. We'll sort it out. I didn't mean to yell.'

He'd do anything to stop her from looking like that—as if the world had come to an end, as if there was no joy and laughter, dancing and champagne, warm summer nights and lazy kisses left in the world. As if all those things had been taken away from her.

'Meg?'

Finally she glanced up. He had to suck in a breath. Her pain burned a hole though his chest and thickened his throat. He dragged in a breath and blinked hard.

She lifted her chin and very gently moved out of his grasp. The abyss inside him grew.

'I'm sorry, Ben. What I asked Dave to do was unfair. I thought it would prove one way or the other whether you were ready for fatherhood.'

'I know you're worried. I can repeat over and over that I'm committed to all of this, but I know that won't allay your fears.' And he was sorrier than he could say about that.

'No.' She twisted her hands together. 'You've never lied to me before. It shows an ungenerosity of spirit to keep testing you as I've done. Your word should be good enough for me. And it is. I do believe you. I do believe you'll stay.'

He eyed her for a moment. He wanted her to stop whipping herself into such a frenzy of guilt. This situation was so new to both of them. 'You don't need to apologise. You're trying to do what's best for the baby. There's no shame in that. Let's forget all about it— move forward and—'

'Forget about it? Ben, I *hurt* you! I can't tell you how sorry I am.'

She didn't have to. He could see it in her face.

'I let you down and I'm sorry.'

And how many times had he let *her* down over the years? Leaving her to deal with Laurie and

Elsie on her own, expecting her to drop everything when he came home for a few days here and there, not ringing for her birthday.

'Although I don't think it's necessary, apology accepted.'

'Thank you.'

She smiled, but it didn't dispel the shadows in her eyes or the lines of strain about her mouth. His stomach dropped. *If I ever lost your friendship.* His hands clenched. It wouldn't happen. He wouldn't let it happen.

Music and laughter drifted down to them from the marquee. The lights spilling from it were festive and cheerful. Out here where he and Meg stood cloaked in the shadows of the garden, it was cool and the festivities seemed almost out of reach.

He swallowed and shifted his weight. 'You want to tell me what else is wrong?'

She glanced at him; took a step back. 'There's nothing.'

Acid filled his mouth. 'Don't lie to me, Meg.'

She glanced away. With her face in profile, her loveliness made his jaw ache. He stared at her, willing her to trust him, to share what troubled her so he could make it better. She was so lovely...and hurting so badly. He wanted—*needed*—to make things right for her.

She took another step away from him. 'Some things are better left unspoken.'

He wasn't having that. He took her arm and led her to a garden bench in the front yard. 'No more secrets, Meg. Full disclosure. We need to be completely open about anything that will affect our dealings with each other and the baby.' He leaned towards her. 'We're friends. Best friends. We can sort this out.'

She closed her eyes, her brow wrinkling and her breath catching.

'I promise we can get through anything.' He tried to impart his certainty to her, wanting it to buck her up and bring the colour back to her cheeks, the sparkle to her eyes. 'We really can.'

She opened her eyes and gazed out at the bay spread below them. 'If I share this particular truth with you, Ben, it will freak you out. It will freak you out more than anything I've ever said to you before. If I tell you, you will get up and walk out into the night without letting me finish, and I don't think I could stand that.'

She turned and met his gaze then and his stomach lurched. Some innate sense of self-preservation warned him to get up now and leave. Not just to walk away, but to run. He ignored it. This was Meg. She needed him. He would not let her down.

'I promise you I will not leave until the conversation has run its course.' His voice came out hoarse. 'I promise.'

Her face softened. 'You don't know how hard that promise will be to keep.'

'Another test, Meg?'

'No.'

She shook her head and he believed her.

Her hands twisted together in her lap. She glanced at him, glanced away, glanced down at her hands. 'I love you, Ben.'

'I love you too.' She had to know how much she meant to him.

She closed her eyes briefly before meeting his gaze again. She shook her head gently. 'I mean I've fallen in love with you.'

The words didn't make sense. He stared, unable to move.

'Actually, fallen is a rather apt description, because the sensation is far from comfortable.'

He snapped back, away from her. *I've fallen in love with you.* No! She—

'I didn't mean for it to happen. If I could make it unhappen I would. But I can't.'

'No!' He shot to his feet. He paced away from her, then remembered his promise and strode back. He thrust a finger at her. *'No!'*

She stared back at him with big, wounded eyes. She chafed her arms. He slipped his jacket off and settled it around her shoulders before falling back on the seat beside her.

'Why?' he finally croaked. He'd done his best to maintain a civilised distance ever since that kiss.

'I know.' She sighed. 'It should never have happened.'

Except...that kiss! That damn kiss on the beach. In the moonlight, no less. A moment of magic that neither one of them could forget, but...

'Maybe it's just pregnancy hormones?'

She pulled his jacket about her more tightly. 'That's what I've been telling myself, trying to will myself to believe. But I can't hide behind that as an excuse any longer.'

'Maybe it's just lust?'

She was silent for a long moment. 'Despite what you think, Ben, you have a lot more to offer a woman than just sex. I've been almost the sole focus of your attention this last month and a half and it's been addictive. But it's not just that. You've risen to every challenge I've thrown your way. You've been patient, understanding and kind. You've tried to make things easier for me. And I can see how much you already care for our child. You have amazed me, Ben, and I think you're amazing.'

His heart thumped against his ribs. If this were a movie he'd take her in his arms right now and declare his undying love. But this wasn't a movie. It was him and Meg on a garden bench. It was a nightmare!

His tie tightened about his throat. His mouth dried. He swallowed with difficulty. He might not be able to declare his undying love to her, but he could do the right thing by her.

'Would you like us to get married?'

'No!'

Ordinarily her horror would have made him laugh. He rolled his shoulders and frowned. 'Why not? I thought you said you love me?' Wasn't marriage and babies what women wanted?

'Too much to trap you into marriage! God, Ben, I know how you feel about marriage. The crazy thing is I would turn my nice, safe world upside down if it would make any difference. I'd follow you on your round-the-world yacht voyage, wait in some small village in Bhutan while you scaled a mountain, go with you on safari into deepest darkest Africa. But I know none of those things will make a difference. And, honestly, how happy do you think either one of us would be—you feeling trapped and suffocated and me knowing I'd made you feel that way?' She shook her head. 'A thousand times no.'

He rested his elbows on his knees and his head in his hands. His heart thudded in a sickening slow-quick rhythm in his chest. 'Would you like me to leave town? It'll be easier if you don't have to see me every day.'

'I expect you're right.'

He closed his eyes.

'But while that might be best for me, it's not what's best for the baby. Our baby's life will be significantly richer for having you as its father. So, no, Ben, I don't want you to leave.'

He stared. She'd told him he was amazing, but she was the amazing one. For a moment he couldn't speak. Eventually he managed to clear his throat. 'I don't know how to make things better or easier for you.'

She glanced down at her hands. 'For a start you

can promise not to hate me for having made a hash of this, for changing things between us so significantly.'

He thrust his shoulders back. 'I will never hate you.' He and Meg were different from his parents. He lifted his chin. They would get their friendship back on track eventually.

'I expect I'll get over it sooner or later. I mean, people do, don't they?'

It had taken her father twenty years. He swallowed and nodded.

She turned to him. 'It's four months before the baby is due. Can we…? Can we have a time-out till then?'

She wanted him to stop coming round? She didn't want to see him for four months? He swallowed. It would be no different from setting off on one of his adventure tours. So why did darkness descend all around him? He wanted to rail and yell. But not at Meg.

He rose to his feet. 'I'll go play host for the rest of the evening. I'll help with the clean-up tomorrow and then I'll lock Elsie's house up and go.'

'I'm sorry,' she whispered.

'No need.'

'Thank you.'

He tried to say *you're welcome*, but he couldn't push the words out. 'If you want to retire for the night I'll take care of everything out here.'

'I'll take you up on that.'

She handed him back his jacket, not meeting his eyes, and his heart burned. She turned and strode towards the house. He watched her walk away and it felt as if all the lights had gone out in his world.

Ben moved into a unit in Nelson Bay. He should have moved further away—to the metropolis of Newcastle, an hour away and an easy enough commute—but he couldn't stand the thought of being that far from Meg. What if she needed help? What if she needed something done before the baby came? She knew he was only a phone call or an e-mail away.

When he'd told her as much the day after the wedding she'd nodded and thanked him. And then she'd made him promise neither to ring nor e-mail her—not to contact her at all. He'd barely recognised the woman who'd asked that of him.

'It shouldn't be that hard,' she'd chided at whatever she'd seen in his face. 'In the past you've disappeared for months on end without so much as a phone call between visits.'

It was true.

But this time he didn't have the distraction of the next great adventure between him and home. Was this how Meg had felt when he'd left for each new trip? Worried about his safety and concerned for his health?

Always wondering if he were happy or not?

He threw himself into preparations for the big things he had planned for his future—things he'd only hinted to Meg about. Plans that would cement his financial future, and his child's, and integrate him into the community in Port Stephens.

But somewhere along the way his buzz and excitement had waned. When he couldn't share them with Meg, those plans didn't seem so big, or so bright and shining. He'd never realised how much he'd counted on her or how her friendship had kept him anchored.

Damn it all! She'd gone and wrecked everything—changed the rules and ruined a perfectly good friendship for something as stupid and ephemeral as love.

On the weekends he went out to nightclubs. He drank too much and searched for a woman to take his mind off Meg—a temporary respite, an attempt to get some balance back in his life. It didn't work.

I don't like the way you treat women.

Whenever he looked at a woman now, instead of good-time sass all he saw was vulnerability. He left the clubs early and returned home alone.

'Oh, you have it bad all right,' Dave laughed as they shared a beer one afternoon, a month after Ben had moved into his apartment in Nelson Bay.

Ben scowled. 'What are you talking about?' He'd hoped a beer with his friend would drag his mind from its worry about Meg and move it to more sensible and constructive areas, like fishing and boating.

'Mate, you can't be that clueless.'

He took a swig of his beer. 'I have no idea what you're talking about.' Did Dave think he was pining for greener pastures and new adventures? He shook his head. 'You've got it wrong. I'm happy to be back in Port Stephens, and I appreciate all your help over these last couple of months.'

Dave had tipped Ben off about a local eco-tourism adventure company that had come up for tender. There'd been several companies Ben had considered, but this one had ticked all the boxes. Contracts would be exchanged this coming week.

'This new direction I'm moving in is really exciting. I want to expand the range of tours offered, which means hiring new people.' He shrugged. 'But I've a lot of connections in the industry.' He meant to make his company the best. 'These are exciting times.'

Dave leant back. 'Then why aren't you erupting with enthusiasm? Why aren't you detailing every tour you mean to offer in minute detail to me this very minute and telling me how brilliant it's all going to be?'

Ben rolled his shoulders. 'I don't want to bore you.'

'Oh? And sitting there with a scowl on your face barely grunting at anything I say is designed to be entertaining, is it?'

His jaw dropped. 'I…' Was that what he'd been doing?

Dave leaned towards him. 'Listen, ever since you and Meg had that falling-out you've been moping around as if the world has come to an end.'

'I have not.'

Dave raised an eyebrow.

He thrust out his jaw. 'How many times do I have to tell you? We did not have a falling out.'

Dave eyed him over his beer. 'The two of you can't keep going on like this, you know? You have a baby on the way.'

Ben's head snapped back.

'It *is* yours, isn't it?' Dave said, his eyes serious.

Ben hesitated and then nodded.

'You need to sort it out.'

Ben stared down into his beer. The problem was they had sorted it out and this was the solution. He'd do what Meg needed him to do. Even if it killed him.

'Look, why don't you take the lady flowers and chocolates and just tell her you love her?'

Liquid sloshed over the sides of Ben's glass. 'I don't love her!' He slammed his glass to the table.

'Really?' Dave drawled. 'You're doing a damn fine impression of it, moping around like a love-sick idiot.'

'Remind me,' he growled. 'We *are* supposed to be mates, right?'

Dave ignored him. 'I saw the way you looked at her at the wedding. You could barely drag your eyes from her.'

'That's just lust.' Even now her image fevered his dreams, had him waking in tangled sheets with an ache pulsing at his groin. It made him feel guilty, thinking about Meg that way, but it didn't make the ache go away.

Dave sat back. 'If it were any other woman I'd

agree with you, but this is Meg we're talking about. Meg has never been just another woman to you.'

Ben slumped back.

'Tell me—when have you ever obsessed about a woman the way you've been obsessing about Meg?'

She was the mother of his child. She was his best friend. Of course he was concerned about her.

'Never, right?'

Bingo. But…

The beer garden spun.

And then everything stilled.

Bingo.

He stared at Dave, unable to utter a word. Dave drained the rest of his beer and clapped him on the shoulder. 'I'm off home to the wife and kiddies. You take care, Ben. We'll catch up again soon.'

Ben lifted a hand in acknowledgement, but all the time his mind whirled.

In love with Meg? *Him?*

It all finally fell into place.

Piece by glorious piece.

Him and Meg.

He shoved away from the table and raced out into the mid-afternoon sunshine. He powered down the arcade and marched into the nearest gourmet food shop.

'Can I help you, sir?'

'I'm after a box of chocolates. Your best chocolates.'

The sales assistant picked up a box. 'One can't go past Belgian, sir.'

He surveyed it. 'Do you have something bigger?'

'We have three sizes and—'

'I'll take the biggest box you have.'

It was huge. Tucking it under his arm, he strode into the florist across the way. He stared in bewilderment at bucket upon bucket of choice. So many different kinds of flowers…

'Good afternoon, son, what can I get for you?'

'Uh…I want some flowers.'

'What kind of flowers, laddie? You'll need to be more specific.'

'Something bright and cheerful. And beautiful.' Just like Meg.

'These gerberas are in their prime.'

The florist pointed to a bucket. The flowers were stunning in their vibrancy. Ben nodded. 'Perfect.'

He frowned, though, when the florist extracted a bunch. They seemed a little paltry. The florist eyed him for a moment. 'Perhaps you'd prefer two bunches?'

Ben's face unclouded. 'I'll take all of them.'

'All six bunches, laddie?'

He nodded and thrust money at the man—impatient to be away, impatient to be with Meg. He caught sight of a purple orchid by the till that brought him up short. A perfectly formed orchid that was beautiful in its fragility—its form, its colour and even its shape. It reminded him vividly of Meg on the night of the wedding.

He'd been such an idiot. He'd offered to marry her when he'd thought marriage was the last thing he wanted. He'd acknowledged that he and she were not his mother and father—their relationship would never descend to that kind of hatred and bitterness. He'd faced two of his biggest demons—for Meg—and still he hadn't made the connection. *Idiot!*

Meg brought out the best in him, not the worst. She made him want to be a better man. All he could do was pray he hadn't left it too late.

The florist handed him the orchid, a gentle smile lighting his weathered face. 'On the house, sonny.'

Ben thanked him, collected up the armful of flowers and strode back in the direction of his car.

His feet slowed as he passed an ice cream shop. Meg couldn't eat prawns or Camembert or salami, but she could have ice cream.

He strode inside and ordered a family-size tub of their finest. His arms were so full he had to ask the salesgirl to fish the money out of his jacket pocket. She put the tub of ice cream in a carrier bag and carefully hooked it around his free fingers.

She placed his change into his jacket pocket. 'She's a lucky lady.'

He shook his head. 'If I can pull this off, I'll be the lucky one.' He strode to his car, his stomach churning.

If he could pull this off. *If.*

He closed his eyes. *Please, God.*

CHAPTER TWELVE

MEG HEAVED A sigh and pulled yet more lids from the back of her kitchen cupboard. From her spot on the floor she could see there were still more in there. She had an assortment of lids that just didn't seem to belong to anything else she owned. She'd tossed another lid on the 'to-be-identified-and-hopefully-partnered-up' pile when the doorbell rang.

She considered ignoring it, but with a quick shake of her head she rolled to her knees and lumbered upright. She would not turn into her father. She would not let heartbreak turn her into a hermit.

Pushing her hands into the small of her back, she started for the door. Sorting cupboards hadn't induced an early nesting instinct in her as she'd hoped—hadn't distracted her from the hole that had opened up in her world. A hole once filled by Ben.

Stop it!

Company—perhaps that would do the trick?

She opened the door with a ready smile, more than willing to be distracted by whoever might be on the other side, and then blinked at the blaze of colour that greeted her. Flowers almost completely obscured the person holding them. Flowers in every colour. Beautiful flowers.

Then she recognised the legs beneath all those flowers. And the scent of leather and whisky hit her, playing havoc with her senses.

That was definitely distracting.

Her pulse kicked. Her skin tingled. She swallowed. This kind of distraction had to be bad for her. *Very* bad.

She swallowed again. 'Ben?'

'Hey, Meg.'

And she couldn't help it. Her lips started to twitch. It probably had something to do with the surge of giddy joy the very sight of him sent spinning through her.

'Let me guess—you're opening a florist shop?'

'They're for you.'

For *her*? Her smile faded. An awkward pause opened up between them. Ben shuffled his feet. 'Take pity on a guy, won't you, Meg, and grab an armful?'

It was better than standing there like a landed

fish. She moved forward and took several bunches
of flowers out of his arms, burying her face in
them in an attempt to drown out the much more
beguiling scent of her best friend.

She led the way through to the kitchen and set
the flowers in the sink, before taking the rest of the
flowers from Ben and setting them in the sink too.

'Careful,' she murmured, pointing to the stacks
of plastic containers littering the floor.

Every skin cell she possessed ached, screaming
for her to throw herself into his arms. Her fingers tingled with the need to touch him. Ben had
hugged her more times than she could count. He
wouldn't protest if she hugged him now.

Her mouth dried. Her throat ached. The pulse
points in her neck, her wrists, her ankles all
throbbed.

She couldn't hug him. She wouldn't be hugging
him as her best friend. She'd be hugging him as
her dearest, darling Ben—the man she was in love
with, the man she wanted to get downright dirty
and naked with.

And he'd...

She closed her eyes. 'What are you doing here,
Ben?'

When she opened them again she found him
holding out a box of chocolates. 'For you.'

His voice came out low. The air between them crackled and sparked.

Or was that just her?

She took the chocolates in a daze. 'I...' She moistened her lips. 'Thank you.'

A silence stretched between them. She wanted to stare and stare at him, drink in her fill, but she wouldn't be able to keep the hunger from her eyes if she did. And she didn't want him to witness that. She didn't want his pity.

He started, and then held out a bag. 'I remembered you said you'd had a craving for ice cream.'

She set the chocolates on the bench and reached for the ice cream with both hands, her mouth watering at the label on the carrier bag—it bore the name of her favourite ice cream shop.

'What flavour?'

'Passionfruit ripple.'

He'd remembered.

She seized two spoons from the cutlery drawer, pulled off the lid and tucked straight in. She closed her eyes in bliss at the first mouthful. 'Oh, man, this is good.'

When she opened her eyes again she found him eyeing her hungrily, as if he wanted to devour her in exactly the same way she was devouring the ice cream.

She shook herself and swallowed. Maybe he did, but that didn't change anything between them. Sleeping with Ben wouldn't make him miraculously fall in love with her. Worst luck.

She pushed a spoon towards him. 'Tuck in.'

He didn't move. Standing so close to him was too much torture. She picked up the ice cream tub and moved to the kitchen table.

He'd brought her flowers. He'd brought her chocolates. And he'd brought her ice cream.

She sat. 'So, what's the sting in the tail?'

He started. 'What do you mean?'

She gestured. 'You've brought me the sweeteners, so what is it that needs sweetening?'

Her appetite promptly fled. She laid her spoon down. Was he leaving? Had he come to say goodbye?

She entertained that thought for all of five seconds before dismissing it. Ben wanted to be a part of their baby's life. He had no intention of running away.

She went to pick her spoon up again and then stopped. There was still another three months before the baby was due. Maybe he was leaving Port Stephens until then.

It shouldn't matter. After all, she hadn't clapped eyes on him for almost a month.

She deliberately unclenched her hands. *Get over yourself.* He'd only be a phone call away if she should need him.

Need him? She ached for him with every fibre of her being. And seeing him like this was too hard. She wanted to yell at him to go away, but the shadows beneath his eyes and the gaunt line of his cheeks stopped her.

She picked up her spoon and hoed back into her ice cream. She gestured with what she dearly hoped was a semblance of nonchalance to the chair opposite and drawled, 'Any time you'd like to join the party...'

He sat.

He fidgeted.

He jumped back up and put all the flowers into vases. She doggedly kept eating ice cream. It was delicious. At least she was pretty sure it was delicious. When he came back to the table, though, it was impossible to eat. The tension rose between them with every breath.

She set her spoon down, stared at all the flowers lined up on the kitchen bench, at the enormous box of chocolates—Belgian, no less—and then at the

tub of ice cream. Her shoulders slumped. What did
he have to tell her that could be so bad he needed
to give her all these gifts first?

Flowers and chocolates—gifts for lovers. She
brushed a hand across her eyes. Didn't he know
what he was doing to her?

'I've missed you, Meg.'

And his voice…

'I needed to see you.'

She shoved her shoulders back. 'I thought we
had an agreement?' He was supposed to stay away.

Was this a fight she would ever win? Her fingers
shook as she pressed them to her temples. Would
she ever stop needing to breathe him in, to feast
her eyes on him, to wipe those haunted shadows
from his eyes?

I love you!

Why couldn't that be enough?

She dragged her hands down into her lap and
clenched them. 'Why?'

She might not be able to harden her heart against
him, but she could make sure they didn't draw this
interview out any longer than necessary.

'I realised something this afternoon.' The pulse
at the base of his jaw pounded. 'And once I did I
had to see you as soon as I could.'

Her heart slammed against her ribs. Just looking at him made a pulse start to throb inside her. She folded her arms. 'Are you going to enlighten me?'

He stared at her as if at an utter loss. 'I…uh…' He moistened his lips. 'I realised that I love you. That I'm *in love* with you.'

Three beats passed. Bam. Bam. Bam.

And then what he'd said collided with her grey matter. She shoved her chair back and wheeled away from him.

Typical! Ben had missed her and panicked. She got that. But in love with her? Fat chance!

She spun back and folded her arms. 'The Ben I know wouldn't have stopped to get flowers and chocolates if he'd had an epiphany like that. He'd have raced straight over here and blurted it out on the front doorstep the moment I opened the door.'

'Yeah, well, the guy I thought I was wouldn't have believed any of this possible.' He shot to his feet, his chair crashing to the floor behind him. 'The guy I thought I was didn't believe in love. The guy I thought I was would never have thought he could feel so awkward and at a loss around you, Meg!'

Her jaw dropped. She hitched it back up. 'None

of that means you're in love with me. I accept that you miss me, but—'

'Then how about this?'

He strode around the table and shoved a finger under her nose. His scent slugged into her, swirling around her, playing havoc with her senses, playing havoc with her ability to remain upright.

'For the last month all I've been able to think about is you. I'm worried that you're hurting. I'm worried you're not eating properly and that you're working too hard. I'm worried there's no one around to make you laugh and to stop you from taking the world and yourself too seriously. Every waking moment,' he growled.

He planted his hands on his hips and started to pace. 'And then I worry that you might've found someone who makes you laugh and forget your troubles.' He wheeled back to her. 'Are you dating anyone?'

He all but shouted the question at her. For the first time a tiny ray broke through all her doubts. She tried to dispel it. This was about the baby, not her.

'Ben, no other man will ever take your place in our child's affections.'

'This isn't about the baby!' He paced harder.

'Every waking moment,' he growled. He spun and glared at her. 'And then, when I try to go to sleep, you plague my dreams. And, Meg—' He broke off with a low, mirthless laugh. 'The things I dream of doing to you—well, you don't want to know.'

Ooh, yes, she did.

'For these last two and a half months—eleven weeks—however long it's been—I've been feeling like some kind of sick pervert for thinking of you the way I have been. For having you star in my X-rated fantasies. I've struggled against it because you deserve better than that. So much better. It was only today that my brain finally caught up with my body. This is not just a case of out-and-out lust.'

He moved in close, crowding her with his heat and his scent.

'I want to make love to you until you are begging me for release.'

Her knees trembled at his low voice, rich with sin and promise. Heat pooled low in her abdomen. She couldn't have moved away from him if she'd wanted to.

'Because I love you.'

He hooked a hand behind her head and drew her mouth up to his, his lips crashing against hers in a hard kiss, as if trying to burn the truth of his words against her lips.

He broke away before she could respond, before she'd had enough...anywhere near enough.

He grabbed her hand and dragged her towards the back door. 'Where are we going?'

'There's something I want to show you.'

He pulled her all the way across to Elsie's yard, not stopping till they reached the garden shed. Flinging the door open, he bundled her inside.

In the middle of the floor sat a baby's crib. A wooden, hand-turned baby's crib. She sucked in a breath, marvelling at the beauty and craftsmanship in the simple lines. She knelt down to touch it. The wood was smooth against her palm.

'I've been coming here every day to finish it. I wait until you leave for work. I make sure I'm gone again before you get home.'

Her hand stilled. 'You made this?'

Drawing her back to her feet, he led her outside again. He gestured across to her garden. 'Who do you think is taking care of all that?'

For the first time in a month she suddenly realised how well kept the garden looked. She swallowed. It certainly wasn't her doing. She swung to him. 'You?'

'Tending your garden, making that crib for our baby—nothing has filled me with more satisfaction in my life before. Meg, you make me want to be a better man.'

He cradled her face in his hands. She'd never seen him more earnest or more determined.

'I want to build a life with you and our children—marriage, domesticity and a lifetime commitment. That's what I want.' His hands tightened about her face. 'But only with you. It's only ever been you. You're my destiny, Meg. You're the girl I always come home to. I just never saw it till now.'

For a moment everything blurred—Ben, the garden shed, the sky behind it.

'And if you don't believe me I mean to seduce you until you don't have a doubt left. And if you utter any doubts tomorrow I'll seduce you again, until you can't think straight and all you can think about is me. And I'll do that again and again until you do believe me.'

She lifted her hand to his mouth. 'And if I tell you that I *do* believe you?' She smiled. A smile that became a grin. She had to grin or the happiness swelling inside her might make her burst. 'Will you still seduce me?'

That slow, sinfully wicked grin of his hooked

up the right side of his mouth. He traced a finger along her jaw and down her neck, making her breath hitch. 'Again and again and again,' he vowed, his fingers trailing a teasing path along the neckline of her shirt back and forth with delicious promise.

'Oh!' She caught his hand before he addled her brain completely.

'*Do* you believe me, Meg?' His lips travelled the same path his finger had, his tongue lapping at her skin and making her tremble.

'Yes.' She breathed the word into his mouth as his lips claimed hers.

The kiss transported her to a place she'd never been before—to a kingdom where all her fairytales had come true. She wrapped her arms about his neck, revelling in the lean hardness of his body, and kissed him back with everything she had.

It was a long time before they surfaced. Eventually they broke off to drag oxygen into starved lungs. She smiled up at him.

He grinned down at her. 'You love me, huh?'

'Yep, and you love me.'

Was it possible to die from happiness? She shifted against him, revelling in the way he sucked in a breath.

'You want to explain about the flowers and the chocolates?'

The fingers of his right hand walked down each vertebra of her spine to rest in the small of her back, raising gooseflesh on her arms. 'Dave said I should woo you with flowers and chocolates. I wanted to woo you right, Meg.'

She moved in closer. That hand splayed against her back. 'And the ice cream?'

'That was my own touch.'

'It was my favourite bit.'

His lips descended. 'Your favourite?'

'Second favourite,' she murmured, falling into his kiss, falling into Ben. *Her* Ben.

When he lifted his head again, many minutes later, she tried to catch her breath. 'Ben?'

'Hmm?'

'Do you think we can make our next baby the regular way?'

He grinned that grin. Her heart throbbed.

'You bet. And the one after that, and the one after that,' he promised.

* * * * *

Mills & Boon® Large Print
September 2013

A RICH MAN'S WHIM
Lynne Graham

A PRICE WORTH PAYING?
Trish Morey

A TOUCH OF NOTORIETY
Carole Mortimer

THE SECRET CASELLA BABY
Cathy Williams

MAID FOR MONTERO
Kim Lawrence

CAPTIVE IN HIS CASTLE
Chantelle Shaw

HEIR TO A DARK INHERITANCE
Maisey Yates

ANYTHING BUT VANILLA...
Liz Fielding

A FATHER FOR HER TRIPLETS
Susan Meier

SECOND CHANCE WITH THE REBEL
Cara Colter

FIRST COMES BABY...
Michelle Douglas

0813 Rom LP

75